Amado Muro with son in Chihuahua.

THE COLLECTED STORIES
OF
AMADO MURO

Thorp Springs Press

Grateful acknowledgment is made to these magazines in which
all of these stories have appeared in various versions: *The Americas;
The Arizona Quarterly; The Mexican-American* (edited by Amado
Muro); *The New Mexico Quarterly; The Texas Observer;* and the
anthology, *California Heartland* (edited by Gerald Haslam).

Library of Congress Cataloging in Publication Data

Muro, Amado.
    Collected stories.

    I. Title.
Pz4.M9767Co (PS3563.U727) 813'.5'5 78-18406
ISBN 0-914476-82-3
ISBN 0-914476-83-1 pbk.

THORP SPRINGS PRESS
3414 Robinson Ave.
Austin, Texas 78722

TABLE OF CONTENTS

INTRODUCTION

In May 1970, the police of Big Spring, Texas, booked a shabbily dressed middle-aged transient whom they had taken off a freight train, holding him overnight to see if he was wanted anywhere. In his possession they found seaman's papers with a faded photograph of the man when he was younger, and a membership card in the St. Louis Newspaper Guild. In the morning, they released the transient, not knowing that he was a prolific writer whose work was being studied in American universities as a supplement to courses in Mexican-American literature.

The transient was the late American writer who wrote under the pseudonym Amado Muro, and has been described as a man "who seems to have written more good short fiction than any other young Mexican-American" (*The Chicano*, New American Library, 1971), and as "one of the most promising Mexican-American writers" (*Forgotten Pages of American Literature*, Houghton Mifflin, 1970). He was neither young nor Mexican-American. The deception was a gentle one, designed to shield a writer who wanted fame no more than did B. Traven. The writer was Chester Seltzer, 55 years old when he was locked up in Big Spring, self-described as an obscure journalist, and my close friend.

Seltzer rode freight trains, worked in the crops, went to sea, lived on skid rows, sometimes worked on newspapers—and, from the time he was 20 until he was 56, when he died in El Paso, wrote short stories that may be the best that have been written in this country about men on the road and in the fields, at the missions, and in the villages of Mexico.

He wrote of men with "eyes so deep-set that the shadows around them looked like bruises" ("Two Skid Row Sketches," *Arizona Quarterly*, Autumn 1971), whose clothes were "so ragged they tied them on with binder twine" ("Hungry Men," *Arizona Quarterly*, Spring 1967), who "bleached the four-dollar blood bank's finger marks off with Clorox so they wouldn't have to wait six weeks to put down again" ("Night Train to Fort Worth," *The Texas Observer*, September 15, 1967).

He wrote in longhand, often late into the night, working to make words say what he wanted them to say. He discarded what he did not like in crumpled paper that made rooms in which he worked look as if they had been thoroughly ransacked. He agonized to make words right, once writing in a letter, "I'm just finishing one. This is only seven pages and it has taken four months."

Stories of people who live "on the long, dusty streets in Chihuahua that hold more poor Mexicans than jails do" have begun to make Seltzer famous, but if there is ever a movement aimed at a general discovery of the lives of quiet desperation lived in poverty's dim ranks, Seltzer is going to be even more widely read. He was not interested in commercial success, and the basement of the aging two-story house he occupied with his family in the Sunset Heights district of El Paso was filled with manuscripts never offered to any publisher, including countless notebooks with the reportage of a lifetime spent among those whose stories are most often told in the words of others.

He chose not to write his own painful story. As a young newspaperman in Bexar County, Texas, Seltzer stood before a judge and said he did not want to kill anybody. The time was World War II. The judge told Seltzer he would be an instrument of the state, and therefore it would be the state, not him, who was doing the killing. Seltzer thought the distinction would be small consolation for the man he killed. He told the judge, "If you believe that, you need help more than I do." The FBI man asked him where he had gotten his ideas. He had no strong claim of formal religion to fall back on. He knew reporters were supposed to be brash men with press cards stuck in their hats, hard-boiled and hurrying to break the news of the latest murder. He told the FBI man he had gotten his ideas from various sources. He mentioned Tolstoy. The FBI man looked up from his notes and wanted to know where he could get ahold of this Tolstoy. Seltzer told the FBI man that would be hard to do because Tolstoy had been dead for years. He did not wish to cloud Tolstoy's reputation, so he added that Tolstoy had put in his time in the army. The FBI man looked disdainful. He said, "I bet he wasn't an officer."

At Lewisburg Penitentiary, Seltzer worked in the quarry, then on Labor Five breaking rock for a guards' parking lot. He joined a hunger strike against racial discrimination in the prison, and it lasted sixty-six days. The doctor the prisoners called Dr. Faustus force-fed him with a "garden hose" that cut his nostrils, making him breathe like a dog.

When he was released, he went home to Cleveland, where he had grown up in a comfortable home with a father, mother and sister who loved him and whom he loved. His father, Louis B. Seltzer, was the editor of the *Cleveland Press*, an influential figure in American journalism who could have helped him and wanted to help him, could have gotten him another start. But the son had his own life to live, and after a few days he rode off on a freight train, heading West.

It was not the first time nor would it be the last that he would ride the freights, drawn to them by "the lonesome dreary moan of a drag whistling the highball." He would always be fascinated by life on the rails and the hobos he met, like the man who told him:

> In San Luis Obispo, this mission preacher talked for an hour. Finally he said, 'When one more comes to God, you can eat.' Nobody knelt down at the altar though. That made him mad and he said he wouldn't let stiffs out until they nosedived. I'm a ram—not a sheep—so I made him open the door.

"Going Short," *The Mexican-American*, August, 1968

He froze on a Nickel Plate freight when the temperature was 12 below, and he rode a "hot man" out of Tucson until his throat was so dry he could not talk. He rode an empty with open laths toward Fort Worth with snow hitting him in the face, and once he crawled into a length of big-diameter pipe to get out of the rain on a flatcar carrying pipe for a Houston oil company. He knew what it's like to ride behind the Big Jack engine, thundering over a highball stretch so fast the wheels are skipping on the rail joints, and what it's like to ride the tops, and the terrible feeling hanging up there when the train is balling and shaking. He watched out for jackrollers and blindsiders, and the yard bulls, the Denver Bobs and the Texas Slims. And once on a freezing night heading West out of Sierra Blanca, Texas, about a year before Seltzer died, a Texas & Pacific brakeman said, "I can't tell you to ride in there," and smiled and turned away while he climbed into the cab of the diesel, where there was heat and drinking water.

He knew the Rescue Missions and the Midnight Missions, the Sunshine Missions and the Sally's Harbor Lights, and Sister Bessie's Mission, where you got three slices of bread and gravy and unsweetened coffee for breakfast, and a stale doughnut if the bakeries came through.

On New Year's Day, 1970, TV cameramen went to the Salvation Army's Harbor Light Center at 9th and Market Streets in St. Louis to take the pictures of homeless men that are a standard feature of news coverage during the holiday season. Among the unidentified men whose faces were shown to television audiences that evening was "Amado Muro." At the time, his story "María Tepache" (*Arizona Quarterly*, Winter 1969), was being cited in *The Best American Short Stories* as one of the distinctive stories of the year. It is about a poor Mexican shopkeeper who feeds a wanderer too destitute to pay. The listing was one of at least seven he had received in the annual since 1944 when "A Peddler's Notebook," published in *Southwest Review*, was cited. Ironically, his stories were listed in the section reserved for foreign authors publishing in American magazines.

Seltzer chopped bumblebee cotton at Big Spring for 50 cents an hour, made $1.50 topping carrots at Phoenix, picked peaches at Modesto and cotton at Gila Bend, where they would holler "coontail" when they saw a rattlesnake and two Mexicans got bitten in one afternoon. He knew labor camps like Down-the-Road Dugan's and Wild Grass Woodie's and Indian Bill's, and went out with day haulers like Cadillac Jack, Portugee Joe and Uncle Bill, and lived in the Fruit Pickers Cothouse and Red's flophouse with the men who were caught "in the nightmarish cycle of missions, labor camps, freight trains and the law and Sweet Lucy."

He went to sea for awhile, sailing as an ordinary seaman on long trips to Greece and South America. At Corfu, the White Star Line freighter was on the hook about a mile from the wharves when a group of affluent Greeks came out to confer with the captain, who was a Greek. On that particular day, he was mopping up on the sanitary detail. The visitors were in the fore-castle and not knowing this he blundered in with his mop and bucket. The captain ordered him out and in making his exit he inadvertently spilled soapy water on the shoe of one of the visitors. The captain upbraided him crudely. His pride injured, he wrote a poem about the captain. The ending went:

With an ice pack for a pillow and a straitjacket for a bed
He'll lie supine as his keepers gently massage his head
For he is not a normal man. He delights in discord and strife
And a lunatic asylum is the proper stage for his life.

He gave the poem to a friend, Louie, an oiler, who posted it on the bulletin board, breaking a promise not to do this until the ship docked at New Orleans. The 25-day return trip on the old Liberty ship was a Calvary for him. He recalled the poem as his only literary success since the seamen said they liked it.

In between times, he worked on newspapers, at least fifteen of them, including the *St. Louis Post-Dispatch*. He worked in, among other towns, Las Cruces, New Mexico; San Diego and Bakersfield, California; New Orleans, Louisiana; Prescott, Arizona; and Dallas, San Antonio, Galveston, Wichita

Falls and El Paso, Texas. While working for the El Paso *Herald-Post* in the 1940s he met and married Amada Muro, a native of Chihuahua City, Mexico, who had grown up in El Paso. He adopted a variation of his wife's maiden name as his pseudonym. In the later years of their marriage, Amada and their two sons lived in El Paso while he traveled the railroads and farm fields, taking notes or, when money ran low, sought employment on a newspaper, going to a distant city while his family stayed home.

Of newspapering, he said, "All I want is a place where they have a Y and a mission or railroad yards." He liked to punch the light bag, run and work out with weights. He was a strong man, big enough to have boxed as a lightheavyweight, and he could still do 235 pounds on the bench press when he was in his fifties; he said it consoled him for growing old. Toward the end of his life, a newspaper in Decatur, Illinois, needed a wire editor. He sent them his résumé and they wrote back, interested. They also sent him a handbook of regulations. "It banned use of newspaper stationery," he wrote in a letter, "and said whistling or 'wrestling' in the office was cause for dismissal. It had strictures on dress, wearing a tie and suit, and not doing outside work of any kind, including writing, unless granted permission by one's supervisor. Nothing was said about the newspaper's policy or ideas on news-gathering so I concluded the trivial was more important than a newspaper's main objectives and thought it was a good place to stay away from. I've never wrestled in a newspaper office. I've whistled, though—sometimes even hummed, so wouldn't be much of a prospect."

The managing editor of a California newspaper assigned him to write editorials. Another war came along, this one in Southeast Asia. It was not until the war had gone on for a few years that there was growing resistance to it and to the toll of lives. From the beginning, he was against it. Of students who early opposed the war, he wrote in an editorial, ". . . they make up a moral force any nation should be proud of." It was not popular at that time to say that sort of thing, and what he wrote outraged many, including some who called him a Communist. "The funny thing," he said, "is I only met one Communist in my life—when I was covering the waterfront in New Orleans, and we discussed a seamen's strike, not ideologies." The owners of the newspaper supported the nation's intervention in Southeast Asia. They told him to dig in on the war protesters. He refused, and another man took his place on the editorial page.

His stories found a home in university quarterlies. While he rode the Texas & Pacific freights to Big Spring and chopped cotton, his stories appeared in prestigious literary magazines. They sometimes paid him $20 or $25 a story, but more often paid nothing, as is the custom.

Eventually the anthologies found him, and in the last years of his life his stories appeared with regularity in collections, at least two of which were used as supplementary texts at the University of Texas at El Paso where his oldest son, Charles, graduated with a B.A. in English in 1973 and his younger son, Robert, graduated with a B.A. in Journalism in 1976. He told his wife Amada he did not write to become famous, that he wrote because he liked to write, that he wrote for his own satisfaction.

On a hot July morning in El Paso three months before he died, a morning of the kind he liked to say fitted a man for work as one of Hell's gate-tenders, we sat talking for the last time. The talk turned to old times in Mexico. Once in Mexico City, he recounted, he sat with only a few pesos in his pocket, having breakfast on the balcony of a café on the Zócalo, sipping the strong *café con leche* that is a meal in itself, a newspaper unfolded beside him on the table. Looking out on people stirring peacefully in early morning sunlight, hopefully starting a new day, he said to himself, "Chester Seltzer, you are the luckiest man in the world."

On a Sunday morning early in October 1971, he died of a heart attack at Zamora's News Stand on Paisano Drive in El Paso. He had gone there to look at magazines from Mexico City, and to talk. Two days later we buried him in El Paso's Evergreen Cemetery, which is bordered by the main railroad lines. It was a fresh fall day, with gray clouds drifting in a muted sky and a light breeze blowing. He had intended to "catch out" that morning for Odessa, 280 miles down the tracks.

AY, CHIHUAHUA!

My Uncle Rodolfo Avitia was a burly man with herculean shoulders and a booming bass voice. He wore his heavy gray moustache in the style popularized by the pulque venders in Porfirio Diaz's day, and he never went out without clamping his big Zacatecas sombrero on his massive head.

The mustache and the sombrero were his only obvious vanities. But he had still another. My uncle was very proud of being Chihuahuan. He was proud of everything related to his native state, and intolerant of anyone who tried to discredit either Chihuahua or its people.

Did feminine beauty exist outside Chihuahua? Not for my Uncle Rodolfo. For him, Chihuahuan women were many times lovelier than those from Jalisco, who are popularly believed to be the most beautiful in all Mexico. His extravagant opinions on this subject, expressed at the slightest provocation—more often without any provocation at all—made the ladies in our neighborhood, Chihuahuans all, beam gratefully at Uncle Rodolfo.

And so it was in all things. Could a Mexican born in a state other than Chihuahua become a boxer worthy of the name? My uncle said not. Could anyone but a Chihuahuan be a success in the bull ring? Uncle Rodolfo thought it most unlikely. Could a statue be fashioned with beauty and artistry by craftsmen from any place but Chihuahua? "No," said my Uncle Rodolfo.

Aware of his invincible opinion that no Mexican of integrity would allow himself to be born anywhere but in Chihuahua,

I was not at all surprised when he told me that a swineherd from Chihuahua was the only Mexican ever to get to heaven under his own power.

He told me about this resourceful Chihuahuan on the night of my tenth birthday, after the *piñata* had been broken. As an afterthought he added that if I behaved better, I would stand a good chance of being the second Chihuahuan to enter heaven.

"Who was that first man?" I asked, already picturing myself as the second.

"Pedro Urdemales," my uncle said. "He was the greatest rogue in all Mexico. Like you, he was born in Hidalgo del Parral, which is, as you know, Mexico's most delightful spa."

I wanted to know all about how Pedro Urdemales got into heaven. So my uncle opened a bottle of Cruz Blanca beer, which is made in Chihuahua, and sat down. This is the story as he told it:

Although Pedro Urdemales was born in Hidalgo del Parral, at an early age he went to Tórreon, in Coahuila State, to be a swineherd in a cotton-growing section of Mexico known as La Laguna.

Over the years the Devil kept track of this rascal of a swineherd with keen and admiring interest. When he heard that Pedro Urdemales had died, he ordered his imps to build a welcoming blaze and stepped into his brimstone palace to wait. Pedro was not long in arriving. Like the good Chihuahuan he was, he walked into hell singing the praises of his home town at the top of his lungs:

> *Ay, Hidalgo del Parral, Chihuahua,*
> *Tierra en donde vi la luz,*
> *No me alboroten el agua,*
> *Hijos de la Santa Cruz.*

When he finished his song, Pedro knocked boldly at the Devil's door.

"Who is it?" the Devil barked.

"It's me, Pedro Urdemales."

When he heard Pedro's voice, the Devil rushed out, sprang to his prickly-pear throne, and commanded his imps to pour boiling water on Pedro's head. Impassive as ever, Pedro took off his hat, shook it a few times, and squeezed out the steaming water.

"That little shower was just like the kind we used to have back up in Chihuahua," he remarked pleasantly.

The Devil gritted his teeth. He hollered to the imps to pile more green live-oak wood on the fire. The flames shot up like orange lances. Knowing that his kingdom had never been hotter, the Devil grinned maliciously and asked Pedro how he liked it.

"Well, it *is* a little warm," Pedro conceded. "It reminds me of the days when I was herding hogs back up in La Laguna."

The Devil flew into a rage. He ordered his imps to poke him with their pitchforks. But Pedro only laughed and said it reminded him of the time he had run after a rattlesnake into a prickly-pear thicket outside of Parral.

At that the Devil sprang from his throne and ground his cloven hoofs in the blazing coals of his kingdom. He rushed over to Pedro and led him into the kitchen, which is and was the hottest room in all hell. "If you won't suffer outside, then suffer in here," he snarled.

Pedro took a long look around. "Warm," he remarked. "It's like a midsummer day back up in Parral, where I was born. Then, too, it isn't much cooler than it was when I was herding hogs in La Laguna."

The Devil bellowed at Pedro never to mention Parral or La Laguna again. He was tired of hearing about them.

"Cook," said the Devil, pushing Pedro toward the brimstone stove.

So Pedro fried beans and made fat tortillas, just as the women had made them back up in Parral. He had even smuggled in some red pepper to flavor the beans. As Pedro cooked, he sang lustily. From his brimstone palace, the Devil could hear him. Since he doted on long, mournful faces, he winced and clapped his hands to his ears. But Pedro's voice cut through the Devil's defending hands and thundered in his ears.

> *Gritaba Francisco Villa,*
> *En la estacion de Calera,*
> *Vamos a darle la mano*
> *a Don Pánfilo Natera.*
>
> *Ahora si, borracho Huerta,*
> *Haras las patas mas chuecas*
> *Al saber que Pancho Villa*
> *ha tomado Zacatecas.*

The Mexican imps began to shout "Viva Villa." After a while imps from other nations laid down their shovels, and they too began to shout "Viva Villa," with European, Asiatic, American, and African accents.

The Devil's discipline was shattered, but our Chihuahuan friend wasn't through yet. The dinners Pedro served made the Mexican imps happy and content with their lot, something previously unheard of in hell. But the non-Mexican imps suffered far beyond their normal quotas. The peppers blistered their lips, and after a few days of Pedro's cooking they all began to lose weight. The Devil asked Pedro why.

"I don't know." Pedro said. "It can't be the peppers. Why, back home in Parral all of us grew up on really fiery peppers. What I've been giving the imps can't compare with them."

But the Devil continued to question Pedro, and finally Pedro told him: "They're unhappy because they have nothing to wear. They're envious of the angels with their long white robes."

Pedro even volunteered to make shirts for the imps, and after a while the Devil agreed. So the Chihuahuan settled down to the job of making shirts.

He sewed a big red cross on the back of each. When the Devil and his imps saw the crosses, they scattered frantically, and Pedro was free to climb up to the golden gates of heaven.

He knocked and knocked. Finally he heard St. Peter ask: "Who's there?"

"It's me, Namesake. It's Pedro Urdemales, who was born in Parral not far from the bridge of Guanajuato and who later lived in La Laguna."

"Go away," St. Peter called out.

"Why, Namesake?" Pedro Urdemales asked.

"Pedro Urdemales," St. Peter said sternly, "two days before your death you killed all the hogs you were herding and sold them. You cut off the tails, stuck them in the swamp, and told your boss the hogs had bogged down. You showed him their upthrust tails as proof. You deceived your boss not once but many times. There is no place for you in heaven."

"Look, Namesake," Pedro said, "it's nice and cool up here, just as it is down in Santa Bárbara—that's a town near Parral—and all I want is a look at this beautiful place so I can tell others about it."

St Peter, tired of the servility most people assumed in his presence, warmed to Pedro Urdemales. So he opened the gates of heaven a little. Pedro stuck his finger in the tiny opening. "Namesake, the wind blew my sombrero off. Let me come in and find it."

"All right," St. Peter agreed, "but you've got to leave as soon as you find your hat."

A month went by, and Pedro Urdemales still had not made his requested departure from heaven. Meanwhile, angels complained of mysterious losses. Some of them reported missing feathers and rings. Others said their golden crowns had disappeared. They told the Lord of these strange happenings. "You must be mistaken," He said, "There can be no dishonesty here."

But the complaints grew in both intensity and number. Finally the Lord called St. Peter before him. It was then that St. Peter admitted that he had let a Mexican swineherd named Pedro Urdemales pass through the gates of heaven to look for his hat.

A party of angels set out to hunt for Pedro, but he could not be found. Finally the Lord called a messenger angel to his side. He said: "I want you to fly down to earth and find a Mexican, a peon wearing a big sombrero, and bring him to me."

The angel flapped his wings and flew away. An hour later he came back carrying a Mexican.

"Where did you find him?" the Lord asked.

"I flew all the way to Mexico City," the messenger angel said. "On Avenida Juarez I didn't see a single man like the one you described. All wore U.S. style hats and carried brief cases. I was tired of flying, so I made myself invisible and got on a second-class bus marked 'La Merced.' A man in the back of the bus had a guitar under his arm. After about a block, he sprang from his seat and started to sing:

> *Si Adelita se casara con Carranza*
> *Y Pancho Villa con Alvaro Obregòn,*
> *Yo me casaba con Adelita*
> *Y se acababa la revolucìon."*

The Lord smiled, "What did the other passengers do while he was singing?" He asked.

"They all began shouting 'Viva Villa,' " the messenger angel replied.

The smile on the Lord's face broadened as He turned to the Mexican and asked, "What is your name?"

"Emilio de la Rosa, here to serve you, my Lord."

"Do you know a song called *Corrido del Norte?*"

Emilio de la Rosa nodded happily.

"Then sing it," the Lord commanded.

Emilio squared his shoulders, threw back his head, and sang out as loudly as he could.

> *Yo les aseguro que soy Mexicano*
> *De acà de este lado,*
> *Porque uso de lado sombrero vaquero*
> *Y fajo pistola, chamarra de cuero,*
> *Y porque me acostumbro cigarro de hoja*
> *Y anudo mi cuello con mascada roja*
> *Se creen otra cosa.*

The angels, all non-Mexicans, flapped their wings in time and tapped their toes on the clouds. There was a collective gasp as a big sombrero came spinning toward them, raising a milky dust.

"*Ay Chihuahua, cuanto Apache,*" a voice shouted. "*Viva Mexico! Viva Felipe Angeles! Vivan los dorados de Villa!*"

The Lord smiled as Pedro Urdemales hurdled a cloud and sprang into view. He nudged St. Peter and said: "I knew there wasn't a Mexican anywhere who could hear that song and keep quiet."

Then the Lord turned to the messenger angel and asked him to fly Emilio de la Rosa back to Mexico City.

"Lord," Emilio de la Rosa said, "if you'll tell him to drop me off somewhere in the Colonia Zapata I'll be very grateful. At this hour the buses on Avenida Juarez are crowded and I have to transfer twice to get to the Colonia Zapata."

"To the Colonia Zapata," the Lord ordered the angel.

"*Adiòs, paisa',*" Pedro Urdemales shouted as the messenger angel placed Emilio de la Rosa on his back. "Many thanks for the song."

The Lord smiled at Pedro, took him by the scruff of the neck, and led him out of heaven. As the gates closed behind him, Pedro leaped into space and that was the last that was ever seen or heard of him. Except in Chihuahua, where stories about him have been told ever since, according to my Uncle Rodolfo.

SUNDAY IN LITTLE CHIHUAHUA

When I was a boy, not long up from Parral, I lived with my uncle Rodolfo Avitia, my mother Amada Avitia de Muro, and my sisters Consuelo and Dulce Nombre·de Maria in the quarter called "Little Chihuahua" on the El Paso side of the Rio Grande.

Next door to the tenement in which we lived was a tiny café called "La Perla de Jalisco." This café was run by Doña Antonia Olvera, a jolly and industrious woman from Guadalajara, who was known throughout the neighborhood as Toña *"la tapatia,"* as her townspeople are called in Mexico.

Doña Antonia kept busy all day long, humming the *Mexican Hat Dance* while she worked. Her café specialized in dishes that were seldom found elsewhere in Little Chihuahua. Toña *la tapatia* served the sugar tamales that make Oaxaca mouths water. She made the delicate, wispy tortillas, the largest and thinnest in all Mexico, that are among the great prides of Sonora. When a man tired of eating the thick, freckled tortillas of flour made by Chihuahua housewives, he would go to "La Perla" for an agreeable change, secure in the knowledge that not even the tortilla factories could equal Doña Antonia's products in fineness or texture.

Then, too, Toña served *café con leche* just as they do in the Mexico City cafés, with each cup of coffee more than half filled with boiling milk. Where, if not to "La Perla," would a man seeking a cup of hot *champurrado*, made of corn and chocolate, go on a cold winter night? And was anyone ever known to impugn the quality of the tripe which Doña Antonia put into her steaming *menudo*, a stew known to every border Mexican as the only sure cure for a hangover?

"La Perla de Jalisco" was a neat and clean café. On each immaculate table a small dish of *chile bravo* could always be found, and over the front door hung a picture of Juventino Rosas, who, besides being the composer of *Sobre las Olas*, was a *tapatío* himself.

At a front table Toña's husband, Don Ignacio Olvera, sat all day long with his books of philosophy and his bullring reviews stacked up in neat piles before him. He was the president of the "José y Juan" bullfight club and also acted as border correspondent for *El Redondel*, a bullfight magazine published in Mexico City. For his literary service, Don Ignacio received no money at all. But he did obtain passes to the fights in Ciudad Juárez each Sunday, and the satisfaction of seeing the name "I. Olvera, correspondent" at the end of his numerous and popular articles.

Between his exhaustive studies of Plato, whom he referred to as the "Divine Greek," and his equally exhaustive studies of the matador Rafael Gómez, "El Gallo [The Rooster]," whom he referred to as the "Divine Baldhead," he managed to earn a scholar's reputation for himself in the quarter.

Don Ignacio Olvera was a short, pudgy man with deeply imbedded eyes that kept blinking constantly as though trying to beat their way out of the morass of soggy flesh that surrounded them. His cheekbones were smothered beneath puffs of suety skin that made his round face appear boneless. To the genteel residents of our quarter he was known as "The Belly" because of his bobbling paunch. But the more robust residents of Little Chihuahua knew him as "Jiggle Hips," a nickname inspired by his elephantine backside, which swayed like a woman's when he walked down the street.

Don Ignacio sat in the café all day long playing *Novillero* and Agustin Lara's *Silverio* over and over again on the jukebox while he pored over metaphysical disquisitions and bullfight reviews, gathering material for his long articles dealing with past

and present bullfighters. He also wrote poems dedicated to the
Mexican matadors and these, too, were published in *El Redondel*.

Where was the boy in our quarter who could not recite
the verse about the day Andrés Blando killed the bull "Cuatro
Milpas" with one of the mightiest sword thrusts ever seen in the
Plaza of Ciudad Juárez?

On that day Don Ignacio Olvera wrote:

> *Andrés Blando ha descubierto*
> *Una manera de herir*
> *Que no la comprende nadie*
> *Ni es facil de definir.*
>
> [Andrés Blando has discovered
> A way to wound
> That nobody understands
> And that is difficult to define.]

And what aficionado in Little Chihuahua did not know by
heart the satirical ballad he composed on the day the unhappy
apprentices Juan Estrada, "Gallo," and José Lagares, "El Piti,"
heard the three warning bugles and underwent the humiliation
of seeing the bulls they could not kill returned to the corrals by
the trained oxen?

Of that unlucky day, Don Ignacio had written:

> *No quiero carne del toro*
> *Que Lagares no mató.*
> *La quiero del de Gallito*
> *Que vivo se lo dejó.*
>
> [I don't want the meat of the bull
> That Lagares didn't kill.
> I want it from Gallito's
> That was left alive.]

But despite the popularity of his poems, it was generally
agreed that Don Ignacio's renown rested on a foundation of solid
prose. His most famous article was written on the day the
matador Luis Castro, known in the ring as "The Mixcoac Militiaman," cut the ears, tail, and the hoof of the great bull "Mariposa"

from the herd of San Diego de Los Padres. He described the performance thus:

"[Luis Castro] fights with the gaiety and the abandon of the gypsies who dance nude amid flowering lemon trees in Seville's joyous quarter of San Bernardo, where the great bull killer Pepe Luis Vázquez was born. He smiles at the bull as Othello would have smiled had his blindness not kept him from seeing that his Desdemona was faithful. His vibrant cape rises in a harmonious curve like the swallows which make their nests in the eaves of the church of Omnia Santorum, where Juan Belmonte, 'The Earthquake of Triana,' was baptized.

"Plato nailed to the door of his Academy the disconcerting words 'None shall enter without knowing geometry.' And by his work with the cape and the muleta today our great military man of the bullring won the right to enter the Divine Greek's Academy unchallenged. The red ellipses of his interminable *derchazos*, the moving and deeply poetic circumference of his *pase de pecho*, the semicircular tragedy of his *larga cordobesa,* showed us that Luis Castro, too, knows geometry.

"Today our valiant soldier proved that his heart is as big and as round as that great gypsy moon of which the unlucky poet Garcia Lorca has sung. So he conquered the noble bull Mariposa, who, like all true super-brave bulls, had flies on his face and defenses like the branches of the millennial ahuehuete trees in Chapultepec Park.

"Thales de Mileto would have said that his movements with the cape represented a perfect conjugation of music and geometry. A poet like Ronsard would have said that the rhythm of our soldier's muleta was like the agile and beautiful flight of a bird. Becquer would have said its magic was that of a ballad heard in the mysterious depths of the Moruno Quarter of Santa Cruz de Sevilla at three in the morning, the hour when the hearts of the gypsies stop beating. For Luis Castro's muleta has that suave sweep of which the great Nicaraguan poet has spoken.

"Amiable readers, today I have learned that the smell of a brilliant bullfighter is overpowering. That is because it is im-

pregnated with the odor of greatness. When I saw Luis Castro's
farol de rodillas, I thought that the great Rodolfo Gaona, our
beloved 'Caliph of Leon,' had come out of retirement to tread
the sands of the ring once more. Mariano Azuela was born to
be a great writer. Rafael de Urbino was born to be a great painter.
And 'The Mixcoac Militiaman' was born to be a great matador.

"Luis Castro, my hand is extended to you. You have
brought a new sense of joy, a new sense of danger to the ancient
art of Cuchares. Matador, I salute you. *Olé!* for the profession of
the thousand marvels, the most beautiful of all the fiestas."

On Sundays after the eight o'clock Mass at the church of
San Juan de Los Lagos was over, the children of our neighbor-
hood attended the Pachangas, or entertainment, put on by
Don Ignacio.

This was held in the corral behind the "Perla de Jalisco."
Don Ignacio would get out the brilliant cape which Luis Castro
had presented to him in gratitude for his encomiastic article. He
also got out a muleta which had been given to him by the matador Carlos Vera, "Canitas," in appreciation for an article in
which he had compared the young bullfighter's execution of the
la sernista pass to that of its inventor, Victoriano de La Serna
himself.

On the mornings of the Pachangas Don Ignacio was as
nervous as the bullfighters who await their turns in the Plaza de
Cuatro Caminos in Mexico City. On the nights before, he stiffened his cape with fish jelly and on windy Sundays he weighted
down his muleta with wet sand.

For his Pachangas, Don Ignacio had trained a chow dog
that he called "Mariachi" to charge like a bull. He had taught
the dog to follow the sway of Luis Castro's cape and Carlos
Vera's muleta just as a real bull would from the herd of Corlome.

On the blistering summer Sundays when Mariachi was
listless and came to the lures sluggishly, Don Ignacio heaped
insults upon him. "Son of a bad cow," he reviled him. "Solemn
softly, blind burro, little Sister of Charity."

But on the cold winter Sundays when the dog's body was
throbbing with vigor and he came to the lures with a straight and

true charge, Don Ignacio praised him extravagantly. "This is a great and intelligent bull, a rich bonbon from the herd of Corlome," he gravely informed the children. "Kids, I tell you that this brave bull knows Latin, Greek, German, Sanskrit, and Calo."

Don Ignacio wore heel-less bullfighting pumps during the Pachangas. An ancient *montera*—the traditional bullfighter's hat—battered and frizzled, surmounted his massive head. He cited the dog by patting the hardpan earth with his slippered feet. *"Ay, toro,"* he bellowed at the top of his lungs. "Come, 'little pear in sweet sauce.' "

The dog Mariachi, long since grown accustomed to the vagaries of Don Ignacio's mercurial temperament, would look up at his globular master with a resigned expression. Then after a moment he would begin to paw at the earth with his hind legs just as a real bull would do.

"This one is for all of you," Don Ignacio would then yell as the dog charged the cape his corpulent master held behind him in the beautiful style invented by Romero Freg.

The delighted children would crown each pass with an *"¡Olé!"* They whooped and hollered hilariously as Don Ignacio, puffing and wheezing, lowered himself to his pudgy knees in order to execute the dangerous *cambio a Porto Gayola.*

Don Ignacio always explained the origin of every movement to the excited spectators. "Lads, this one is *la saltillera.* It is so called because it was created by our great fellow countryman, Fermin Espinosa, 'Armillita,' who was also known as the 'Maestro of Saltillo.' "

Most of us had been attending the Pachangas for so long that we knew all of the movements and passes by heart.

"You, Macario Buena," Don Ignacio would shout. "Tell me, who created the *sanjuanera* pass and how did the pass get its name?"

"Luis Procuna, 'El Caballero del Penacho Blanco [The Knight with the White Crest],' invented the pass," a small, poorly dressed boy would answer from somewhere in the crowd.

"He called it *sanjuanera,* because he was born in the San Juan de Letran section in the capital."

Don Ignacio always ended the Pachangas with a suicidal pass of his own invention which he had named *la olverina.* This pass resembled an inverted *manoletina* in which the bullfighter stands with his back to the bull. For years Don Ignacio had been trying to persuade some of Mexico's most noted bullfighters to try it out in the ring. But, recognizing the pass as a certain passport to eternity, they had courteously but consistently refused.

After the Pachangas were over, Don Ignacio always started for the back door of the cafe, ostensibly to wash himself down. But the clamorous cries of the children and the shouts of the men and women massed on the balconies of the adjacent tenements never failed to bring him back.

"The ballad, Don Nacho," the crowd yelled. "The ballad of Niño de La Palma."

"*Ay, María, madre mía,*" Don Ignacio complained every Sunday. "Boys, it's hot as three o'clock in Acapulco, and I swear by our sainted Guadalupana, the Lady of All the World and the Queen of the Skies, that I've got to dress for the bullfight."

But the children and the men and women always disregarded his protests.

"The ballad, Don Nacho," they hollered. "Recite the ballad."

Don Ignacio always ended by shrugging his shoulders and waving everyone into silence. He would take off the dusty montera, throw his head back, and square his shoulders. His stentorian voice, quivering with emotion, pierced the air like the cry of a *flamenco* singer.

All of us had learned poems by Longfellow in the American school, all of us had learned poems by Juan de Dios Peza and Antonio Plaza in our homes, but at that age of our lives no poem we had known could make our hearts beat as fast as did *Las Chuflillas del Niño de La Palma.*

With the throbbing intensity of his bass voice, Don Ignacio

could make us all see the bullfighter of Ronda, son of a shoe-maker and once poor like ourselves, in his great hour of victory at Vista Alegre on the day when the Bank of Spain opened its doors to him. He could make us all hear the cry of the Niño, drunk with the exultation of his triumph, as he called to the brave Campos Varela bull, challenging the fierce animal to charge and to catch him.

> *Vengas o no en busca mía,*
> *Torillo, mala persona,*
> *Dos cirios y una corona*
> *Tendrás en la enfermería.*
> *¡Qué alegria!*
> *¡Cógeme, torillo fiero!*
> *¡Qué salero!*
>
> [Come after me or not,
> Little bull, evil person,
> You will have two candles
> And a garland in the hospital.
> What joy!
> Catch me, proud little bull!
> How graceful!]

The deafening applause would rise over the corral in a thundering tympany. The children would sing and whistle the quick, gay *Diana*. At the Pachangas even the most melancholy of the children were laughing and happy.

Once I remember seeing Juana de la Torre there. She was the ugliest girl in our school, so ugly that even the gentlest girls in our class taunted her and called her "Juana the Female Pig." But on the day I saw her there at the Pachangas she was laughing. I could never remember seeing her laugh before.

There, too, I saw Jesús Zamarrippa. Ordinarily Jesús looked tired and sad. He was then eleven years old and he lived in an earthen-floored hut with eight other members of his family. Already he had spent a year in the tuberculosis ward at the city-county hospital. But at the Pachangas that day Jesús' face was radiant.

After the recitation was over the crowds of jubilant children began to disperse. Standing at the back door of the café, Don Ignacio watched until the last child was gone. I remember him best as he stood there with a smile on his face.

Many years later when I was a young man of twenty, I sat in "La Buena Fe" shoe shop and heard my big, burly Uncle Rodolfo defend Don Ignacio against two of our countrymen who were bitterly damning him as a preposterous poseur, a drone, and a parasite, a pickpocket who lived off his wife. "Shut up, sons of the Great Seven," my aroused uncle told them at last.

He stormed out of the shoe shop and I followed him. We walked down South Stanton Street toward Ciudad Juárez slowly. And I asked my Uncle Rodolfo why he had defended Don Ignacio Olvera against charges that were only too true, and why he had become so angry.

My Uncle Rodolfo looked at me with a sheepish expression. He started to tell me and then suddenly stopped. He took off his big Zacatecas sombrero and ran his hand through his gray hair. "Confound it," my uncle said, flushing with the embarrassment of his struggle to express an emotion that I am sure he considered unmanly.

He kept his brown face averted from mine. After a moment he got the words out. "Son," my uncle Rodolfo said slowly without looking at me. "It is just that Don Nacho can make children laugh."

He clamped his hat back down on his head. Then he looked over at me with a defiant expression as though challenging me to smile back at him in derision.

After that we walked over to Ciudad Juárez to eat *fritanga* and drink a "Chiquita Chihuahua" together.

MY FATHER AND PANCHO VILLA

Many, if not most, of my countrymen try to sing and to play the guitar at one time or another during their boyhood days. I was no exception.

Although most of the people of Little Chihuahua, the Mexican quarter of El Paso, agreed that I sang and played badly, there was one who did not. This was Don Guadalupe González, a powerful man with a thick corded neck and biceps that measured almost seventeen inches. Throughout our neighborhood, he was known as *"Siete Luchas,"* or "Seven Struggles," because of his mastery over many trades. Then, too, because of his heroism as a soldier in the army of General Francisco Villa, Don Lupe was generally regarded as a man "more valiant than twenty on horseback." But aside from Don Lupe I had no steady listeners at all, and my music and songs never seemed to be needed on fiesta days or tamale-party nights. Also, for reasons that were apparent to everyone but myself, I could never find a singing partner.

And so it was that on December 12, the "Day of the Lupes," I trudged the streets of Little Chihuahua alone, with my guitar slung over my shoulder, in a hopeless quest for someone whose saint's day it was and whom I could serenade at the fixed price of ten cents a song. On that day guitar music filled the streets of Little Chihuahua, and the neighborhood's numerous Guadalupes stood on street corners or in the doorways of their homes listening to the *mariachi* musicians. For hours I walked up and down, looking hopefully at every Lupe I passed.

As I walked, I remembered how months before, on the Day of San Juan, I had plodded over the neighborhood looking with the very same lack of success for Juans and Juanas to sing to. I tried to lift my spirits by assuring myself that sooner or later I would find a patriot named Guadalupe who would gladly pay a dime just to hear me sing about Chihuahua and Pancho Villa and the Revolution. But none appeared, and so at the corner of Paisano and Ochoa I moved into a doorway and began to cry.

I had just about cried myself out and was getting ready to throw myself into the search again when the booming voice of a man standing at the door of his home made me turn around sharply.

"Sons of María Morales," the man bellowed. "It's raining in Samalayuca, *qué caray!* Ay, Emalina, it's raining in our corn-fields tonight. There goes a dark-hipped Mexican from the mining town of Parral, a rooster with good spurs, who sings and plays as God commanded. You, Amado, come and salute a friend on his saint's day."

I wiped away my tears with the bright red bandana I had wrapped around my neck to give me the appearance of a genuine *mariachi* and walked toward Don Lupe González. Don Lupe stood smiling and looking down at me. Then he roared: "Emalina, bring a cup of *champurrado* and some *buñuelos* for the *mariachi* —and make sure the *champurrado* is hot."

I walked into Don Lupe's home and sat down under the Aguilar Drug Store calendar that had the big picture of the Virgin of Guadalupe on it. Señora González placed before me a steaming cup of the chocolate-and-cornmeal beverage and a plate of the sweet fritters.

"Amado," Don Lupe said, "today is the Day of the Lupes and I want you to sing the *corrido* of Chihuahua for me just as God commanded."

I smiled—a little wanly, I think.

"Sing!" Don Lupe thundered. "Sing as your father sang when he and I rode with Pancho Villa."

"All right, Don Guada', " I said.

So I sang, and after I had finished I felt less mournful.

"Long live Pancho Madero and death to Pascual Orozco!" Don Lupe yelled. Then he turned to me again. "Amado, I've forgotten the name of it, but sing me the *corrido* that says how Valentín never gave an account of himself."

"The *corrido* of Valentín de la Sierra, Don Guada', " I said.

"That's it, Amado," Don Lupe bawled.

So I sang it. Then I sat there drinking hot *champurrado,* watching the tears stream down Don Lupe's stubbled cheeks and thinking that maybe I had been meant to be a great singer after all.

But it was not really my voice that had made Don Lupe cry.

"Sons of María Morales," he said. "When I hear you sing I think of your father. Ay, that shepherd from Zacatecas—a Mexican right down to the ground." He slapped his knee and laughed until tears welled into his eyes again. "Holy Mother, that fellow was afraid of no one," he said. "Not even of Francisco Villa."

When Don Lupe said that, I forgot all about my singing ambitions and leaned forward quickly.

"Don Guada'," you said that my father was not even afraid of General Villa?" I asked.

"Afraid of Pancho Villa?" Don Lupe barked. "I swear by the pines of Majalca that Jesús Muro would have sent Villa for the groceries."

I looked at Don Lupe. His face was still drenched with tears.

"Emalina, more *buñuelos* for the son of my friend!" Don Lupe shouted. "And for me bring *sotol* and that bottle of Widow Romero tequila." This *sotol* is to the people of Chihuahua what *pulque* is to other Mexicans.

Out in the kitchen I could hear Señora González bustling around and singing at the top of her lungs about what Pánfilo Natera told the Federals.

I began to feel better. All the day's disappointments were

wearing away.

"Your father was not afraid of Villa nor of General Benjamin Argumedo nor yet of Don Pablo González," Don Lupe said.

So I asked Don Lupe how he knew, and he told me.

"All that I am going to tell you took place on a bitter cold night out on the sierras of Chihuahua," he said. "I was there with your father and 'The Buzzard,' 'The Cricket,' and a number of other countrymen whose names I can not now recall—all, like myself, soldiers of Villa.

"On that freezing night, General Francisco Villa had ordered us not to build a fire, an order we had all disobeyed for the purpose of roasting a burro. We sat by the fire eating the burro and listening to Jesús Muro sing and play the guitar. You know that, besides being one of the most famous musicians in Pancho Villa's army, your father was also one of its greatest composers. We were sitting there listening to Jesús when a booming voice drowned out the music. Amado, how that voice thundered! Just to think of it makes my whiskers grow.

"We looked up to see General Francisco Villa sitting on his horse Seven Leagues and glaring down at us with an old spring pistol pointed in our direction.

" 'Sons of I don't know how many mothers!' he shouted. 'Tell me, and quickly, which one of you started that fire?'

"Nobody answered at first. Then, after a moment, your father laid down his guitar and got up. 'My general, I built the fire,' he said.

"Pancho Villa did not say a word.

" 'If we are out here on the mountain looking for death,' Jesús Muro explained, 'why should we skulk in the dark and hide from it? Better to eat the burro, so that at least we'll die with our bellies full.'

"I thought we were dead men after that—until I saw General Villa's face relax and break into a smile.

" 'Look, boys,' he said after a moment, 'the Carranza gang isn't far from here—that much we do know. Eat the burro and put out the fire.' Then he turned to your father again.

'Countryman,' he said, 'what was that song you were singing when I rode up to you?'

"That question made us all nervous again. The song Jesus had been singing, one of his own compositions, was called *Gorra Gacha* (Slouch Cap). It owed its name to the fact that Pancho Villa sometimes wore his hat on the side of his head and slanted down over his eyes like a cap. But when your father told him the name of the song and how it came to be written, Pancho Villa began laughing some more.

" 'Sing it, brother,' he said. 'Only not very loud.'

> *Señores tengan presente,*
> *miran lo que van hacer.*
> *Los señores Carrancistas*
> *se vistieron de mujer.*
> *Mucho cuidado, muchachos,*
> *que ay! viene mi general.*
> *Esto es Don Francisco Villa,*
> *el que ganó en el Parral.*
> [Gentlemen, keep in mind,
> look what they're going to do.
> Carranza's men
> dressed up as women.
> Careful boys,
> for here comes my general.
> This is Don Francisco Villa,
> he who won in Parral.]

"I can still see Pancho Villa's expression when he heard that song, can see his shoulders shake with laughter.

" 'Ay, brother of our race, how you sang it!' Pancho Villa laughed. Then he said, 'Many thanks for the song.' and rode off.

"After that, we all made sure the fire's last embers were out."

When I left Don Lupe's home that night, I did not look for people to sing to. I was no longer unhappy because all the Lupes and the Juans and Juanas before them had ignored me completely.

I could even admit to myself that it was only too true that almost all of the singers in Little Chihuahua had better voices than mine. Better singers they might be, but I did not envy them.

For what other boy in Little Chihuahua—or in all of Mexico, even—had a father so brave he did not even fear Pancho Villa?

MY GRANDFATHER'S BRAVE SONGS

My grandfather Trinidad Avitia, a gray-haired street singer, managed to make a living in Parral, Chihuahua, thanks to his guitar and the saints.

His guitar and the saints had been his best friends since his boyhood—the guitar because listeners said he played it well, the saints because there are so many.

When I was a boy, my grandfather sat on a chair in front of the Elegant Tortilla Café all day long playing his guitar and singing for every countryman who went by. Many tourists paid to hear his songs. But Mexicans celebrating their saints' days were his most numerous listeners by far, and since every day is some saint's day the demand for his songs seldom lagged.

My grandfather worked hardest on the "Day of the Lupes" and the "Day of the Juans." On those days Parral's many Lupes and Juans kept him busy singing from daybreak until long after midnight. And on those days as well as the "Day of the Pepes," the "Day of the Manuels" and many other saints' days besides, he got up long before sunrise to sing the traditional *mañanitas* (little morning songs). He sang these outside the home of the person whose saint's day it was.

Then, too, on stifling summer nights my grandfather sat outside his home in the Manuel Acuña neighborhood singing songs like "Glass Eye, the Highwayman" and "Pancho Villa's Winged Horses" for anyone who cared to listen. Many Chihuahuans always did. On those nights everyone, even elderly women, shouted when my grandfather threw back his head, squared his shoulders and sang: *"Soy Mexicano, soy de Chihuahua. A mi bandera le juré honor."* ("I am a Mexican, I'm from Chihuahua. I swore allegiance to my flag.")

And everyone laughed until tears came when he stopped in the middle of a song to imitate General Francisco Villa. Parral residents swore that no one else in Chihuahua State could imitate Pancho Villa the way my grandfather could. He puffed out his cheeks as though he were playing a trumpet, stroked his spiky gray moustache and shouted: "Boys, don't be afraid of Pancho Murguia's bullets. Just be careful of the holes they make."

My grandmother María de Jesús sang with him on those nights. So did everyone else. They cried *"Ay Chihuahua"* and *"Arribe el Norte"* when my grandfather sang the "brave" songs that northern Mexicans like so well.

Folk heroes like Heraclio Bernal and Valentín de la Sierra rode through my grandfather's songs on those nights. So did revolutionary leaders like Villa, Martin "Guero (Blondie)" Lopez, and Maclovio Herrera. Everyone made up new verses for the song *"La Cucaracha"* and the evenings passed all too swiftly.

These summer-night concerts became so popular that entire families from other neighborhoods came over to hear them. Some came from as far as the María Martínez neighborhood almost two miles away.

Wives of poor miners, without radios or money for shows, always thanked my grandfather after the singing was over. "May the dark virgin protect you and cover you with her mantle," they said. This made my grandfather uncomfortable. But my grandmother beamed with pride.

My grandmother liked Mexican music just as much as my grandfather did. She was a cheery, smiling woman, always laughing and joking with everyone. But sometimes she, too, lost her temper. "I like everyone who walks on these streets of God," she often said with pride in her good nature. But after she said this she bit her lip and added "except American blondies."

My grandmother showed her dislike for blondes every time American women asked my grandfather to sing *"Cielito Lindo"* for them on their sightseeing trips to Parral. He always did. But these street serenades made my grandmother so mad she wouldn't let him in the house. "This home is for Christians," she shouted when my grandfather knocked at the door. "It's not for shameless old flirts who serenade American blondies instead of being content with what our own nation produces."

My grandfather soothed her with music. He sang *"La Madrugada"* over and over until she finally let him in. After these outbursts my grandmother was always contrite. She did her best to make up for them by making *pozole, flautas,* and other foods my grandfather liked. And she even tried to compete with the chic blondes herself. She wore her best Zamora shawl wherever she went and even went so far as to pin a San Juan rose in her graying hair.

Except for these rare discords, my grandfather's work went along harmoniously. He liked the people he sang for and he made friends with them all. But he liked best the listeners who bawled and shouted when he sang Mexico's brave songs.

One of the most enthusiastic of his many admirers was a robust, middle-aged woman who ran the "Divine Strawberry" stand at the Hidalgo market. This was Doña Guadalupe Carmona, nicknamed "Lupe la Generala" because of her fondness for recalling the days when she fought for Pancho Villa. Lupe the General liked to tell my grandfather about her army days. "Ay, Don Trini," she sighed, "How gladly I'd give up my strawberry stand for a chance to hitch up my skirts and fight for Pancho Villa again."

The strawberry vendor was a fierce patriot. No military parade in Parral would have been complete without her. On parade days everyone cheered when the general marched by with a bandoleer strapped around her Amazonian torso and a 30-30 rifle on her shoulder.

A militant scowl harshened her dimpled face while she waddled along with the soldiers. A cornhusk cigarette was tucked between her chapped lips. She never threw it away until time to shout "Viva Madero."

Lupe the General wasn't one of those women who pray to St. Anthony for sweethearts. When my grandfather sang romantic songs like *"Maria Bonita"* for other market vendors, she always begged him to stop.

"Ay Mama Carlota not that one, Don Trini," she moaned. "Sing the brave one about how the federals chased Benito Canales instead." The songs she liked best were revolutionary ballads like the "Wet Buzzard" and the "Three Bald-Headed Women." But she liked songs about manhunts, shootings, and executions almost as well.

My grandfather's brave songs made the General wail and shout. They made her bawl: "Ay Chihuahua, land of brave men, where nobody gets shot in the back." Sometimes they even made her weep with fierce pride in Benjamin Argumedo and other heroes of the brave songs.

Once I asked my grandfather why Lupe the General shouted and cried when she sang and why she always marched with the soldiers. I hadn't been a Mexican very long when I asked this, for I was then not quite nine years old. My grandfather, a veteran observer of our countrymen, smiled at me. "Every Chihuahuan kills fleas in his own way," he explained.

Eduardo Romero, the barber, liked the brave songs as much, if not more, than the fiery General did. Don Lalo Romero was a spindly, myopic man with a haggard face buttressed by bouldery cheekbones. Chihuahuans called him "Green Belly" because he came from the lettuce-growing center of León, Guanajuato.

Always timid and shy as a mustang when he wasn't listening to brave songs, he turned into a ranting patriot fierce as the General herself when he heard them.

He took off his bullseye glasses and defied his customers, Chihuahuans all, every time my grandfather sang "The Defense of Celaya, Guanajuato" for him. "I'm the only real man here because I come from Guanajuato," he boasted loudly. Then he glared challengingly at Chihuahuans waiting for haircuts as though daring them to deny it.

On crisp autumn nights my grandfather went to the old Juan de Dios market quarter with a Saltillo serape slung over his shoulder and his Ramírez guitar tucked under his arm. There he joined a working army of mariachi musicians who filled the old quarter with music all night, and never broke ranks until dawn.

The quarter's boisterous streets, so narrow and crowded that two people could hardly walk side by side, were jammed with outdoor food stands, fruit and vegetable stalls, and shouting vendors.

My grandfather wandered through streets named after poets and patriots, looking for countrymen to sing to. He usually found them near the "Meek Burro" bar. And always he sang Mexico's brave songs for them.

Sometimes he bought me steaming cups of vanilla *atole* at the "Beautiful Indian" refreshment stand. While I drank them he chatted with wandering musicians, street clowns, fire-eaters, magicians and other men who made their living on Parral's streets.

Then, too, on those chilly nights he told me how he used to wander over the states of Chihuahua, Coahuila, and Durango, sometimes on horseback but more often on foot, singing at the village fairs. Those were the days when he sang for such Mexican revolutionaries as Pánfilo Natera, Petronilo Hernández, and even Pancho Villa himself.

"Once General Hernández made me play for almost twenty hours in the plazas, streets, and bars of Santiago Papasquiaro, Durango, along with other members of the Agustín González orchestra," he told me. "He liked our songs so much he made us all travel with his army for a month giving campfire concerts out in the Durango Sierra."

Only once in his life did my grandfather ever try to make a living at anything other than music. This was after the Madero revolution when he went to Flagstaff, Arizona to work as a carpenter.

Many miners and housewives in the Manuel Acuña neighborhood said he could have been rich if he had stayed there. But even in Flagstaff my grandfather couldn't stop singing the songs that make Mexicans shout. He sang them for lonely countrymen and even for the American bosses. He had planned to save his money and bring my grandmother, my mother, and my uncle Rodolfo from Chihuahua to live in the United States. But the brave songs proved his undoing.

"They made me homesick," my grandfather said. "When I sang them I forgot I was earning more money and living better than ever before."

So after six weeks he went back to Mexico where he's been playing the guitar ever since.

SISTER GUADALAJARA

"Son, see that you get there," my mother said ominously before I left for Our Lady of the Thunderbolt School in Parral, Chihuahua, every morning.

After this warning my mother signed the cross and blessed me. Then she looked down Ricardo Flores Magón Street to see if Pug Nose Galindo was coming. If he wasn't, she smiled and watched me go without saying a word. But if he was she took me by the shoulders and made me look her straight in the eyes.

"Show some character, Amado," she told me. "Don't let him influence you."

She kept her hands on my shoulders until Pug Nose got to our house. When he came up to us she let me go and turned her attention to him. My mother did her best to be pleasant to Pug Nose. But her unsmiling greeting always sounded like another warning.

"God's good morning to you, Pancracio," she said, making Pug Nose wince by using his Christian name. "And may you both get to your fourth-grade class today."

His reply was always noncommittal. "If God is served, then we will, Señora," he said. This unsatisfactory answer and the indifferent shrug that went with it made my mother suspicious and restive. It was enough to make her stand in the street with her hands on her hips and watch us until we turned down Ramón Ortiz Street.

My mother had cause for suspicion. Pug Nose Galindo

could think of more reasons for playing hooky than a country Mexican can for going to Chihuahua City. Both Pug Nose and I lived within tobacco-spitting distance of school. But at least once a week we never got there. We went down to the Street of Crazy Women instead. Wandering up and down it was more fun than staying in a classroom.

"It's more educational too," Pug Nose always insisted, and I couldn't help but agree. What we saw and heard there we never forgot. The classroom was different; what we heard there we never remembered. Our teacher, Sister Caridad, nicknamed "Sister Guadalajara," because she talked so much about her hometown, looked at things differently though. She put burro's ears on us and made us sit in front of the blackboard every time we played hooky. But both of us agreed that wearing burro's ears was a small price to pay for our footloose days on the Street of the Crazy Women.

The street that enthralled us so wasn't much to look at. It was just another broken-down street in a mining town that had many like it. But to Pug Nose and me it was an exciting change from our own neighborhood with its poor homes on crooked streets that wound up hillsides. Then, too, in those days the Street of the Crazy Women was a village in itself, northern as the *nopal*. One "Viva Villa" was worth four "Viva Zapatas" there, and its mariachis sang about Blondie López instead of Gabino Barrera.

Chihuahuans said this long street held more poor Mexicans than jails do. Its sights and sounds made them all feel at home. Mesquite wood smoke fogged it. Bawling vendors filled it. Misty vapors from steaming cornmeal drifted down it. There, women vendors scrubbed griddles with maguey fiber brushes and countrymen scrubbed their teeth with their fingers in primitive Mexican village style.

Toward sidehills matted with chaparral, mesquite, and gobernadora stood adobe homes with blessed palms hanging over their doors to keep evil spirits and lightning away. Stumpy cottonwoods, misted with gray veils woven by caterpillars, leaned before them. On fair days the gossiping housewives, whose doings gave the street its name, sat on rush-plaited chairs under the trees, where wrapped in thick mantas woven by High Sierra Indians, they patched *rebozos* in the sunshine. Their conversations were famous. They talked mostly about their husbands. Some said they wished they had gone into the convent instead of getting married. Others disagreed. "Ay Madre, it's better to undress one-horned drunkards than dress plaster saints," they insisted. Sometimes Pug Nose and I listened until they drove us away.

We liked the street vendor's cries too. They merged into a boisterous tympany. There was always something to see, something to listen to on the Street of the Crazy Women. Its sights and sounds filled us up like food. We could never get enough of them. Its amiable vulgarity bewitched us. Action was never lacking. It flared swiftly like summer lightning. There was always a fight to watch or an argument to listen to.

Once we saw two paisanos fighting in village style with Tarahumara *sarapes* in one hand and Zacatecas knives in the other. Tense and crouching like cats getting ready to jump, they circled each other feinting with their eyes and shoulders until someone shouted that the police were coming. When they heard this, they glared at each other and put away their knives reluctantly. Then they slung their heavy *sarapes* over their shoulders and stalked off in opposite directions.

But best of all we liked to sit at the outdoor food stand run by Dolores Juárez, a buxom, smiling woman who wore a ragged button-sweater and a burro-belly sombrero. Nicknamed "Lola la Tamalera," this good-natured woman gave us beef marrow to keep us from getting anemic and smiled at our hooky-playing instead of scolding us for it. Lola the Tamale Vendor called her food stand the "Flowers of Tepeyac" in honor of Our Lady of Guadalupe. She kept it plastered with pasteboard posters that read: "Happy the home where *sotol* is unkown" and "Beans or turkey it don't matter long as it fills you up."

Always smelling of frying chicharrones and of the strong tarry soap miners use, the Flowers of Tepeyac was a haven for

the city's poor. Leathery revolutionaries older than three mountains and withered Señoras who knew prayers to make the Devil
run were among Doña Lola's customers. So were broken paisanos
who slept in wheel packing and car lining at the boil-out jungle
near the Parral River.

Money didn't matter to the cheery Tamalera. Gossiping
while she worked did. Almost anyone's credit was good at the
Flowers of Tepeyac. "Where eight can eat so can ten," Doña
Lola told Pug Nose and me every time we asked for it.

Her Turkey Mole was famous and it didn't cost much. But
she seldom served it, cooking it only when she was in inspired
moods. Her paying customers asked her why she didn't make it
more often. When they did, Doña Lola shrugged her brawny
shoulders. "No one ever expected the great Cervantes to write a
Don Quixote every day," she explained.

The Tamalera was proud of her customers and defended
them with cape and sword. "It's true their bellies hate them
because they can't give them enough work to do," she admitted.
"But they're not like those shameless toreros who rub garlic
under their arms to simulate fever so they won't have to fight.
They all know what it is to wear pants and work for a living. And
they're just as good as the Curros—the only difference is they eat
charamuscas instead of bon-bons at Christmas."

In turn her customers all tried to please her even at the
cost of subduing their most picaresque impulses. Under her re-
fining influence, the Flowers of Tepeyac became noted for
decorous behavior.

This was because its patrons never scratched themselves
when the rubberneck bus went by. Elsewhere on the street,
grimacing paisanos jumped up and unbuttoned their shirts when
the tourist bus hove into sight. The bus stopped to give tourists
a look at Parral's down and outers. The down and outers made
sure they got a good one. Moaning and wailing, gnashing their
teeth and sobbing, they clawed and scratched until the bus driver
cursed and tourists turned their faces away. When pity or disgust
flashed over tourists' faces, these paisanos threw back their heads
and howled like delighted children watching the Mexican comics

Cantinflas or Clavillazo.

But the Flowers of Tepeyac's patrons refrained from this because Doña Lola thought it was unpatriotic as well as unseemly.

"Having a little fun by shocking the tourists is one thing," she told them. "But making our blonde cousins from the Land of Whiskey think that the Demon's fleas infest all Mexicans is another. And no true paisano can sincerely bawl *Viva México!* on September Sixteenth after taking part in such a verminous vaudeville."

Many of Doña Lola's customers were fiercely independent men who wore their rags proudly. Pug Nose and I liked to hear them talk about their "lives and miracles."

There was the atheist Justo Arizmendi, a melancholy man who sold razor blades outside the Martínez de la Torre Market. For hours at a time he sat at the Flowers of Tepeyac trying to prove the skies were empty. His pessimism was so intense he looked like he was going to cry every time a housewife had a baby.

"One more come to suffer," he said mournfully.

Don Justo was then almost sixty years old, but he still talked about dying young. "I'll never make old bones," he sadly predicted. "It's my destiny to die in my youth."

The book he liked best was the Bible despite his atheistic beliefs. "In the Bible the passions are great, the homicides tremendous, and the sins capital," he enthused.

The razor blade vendor couldn't bear the sight of a priest. He shook his head sadly every time one went by. Confessionals made him even sadder. "No priest will ever hear the story of my sinful life," he vowed, beating his fist on the board table.

Hecklers often asked him if there was a heaven as the priests say. When they did, he shrugged his spare shoulders indifferently.

"Such questions are senseless as pockets in shrouds, for what does it matter?" he answered. "If there is a heaven the saints, prophets, and martyrs will rule us there just as rich Mexicans do down here."

Lola la Tamalera didn't like him. She called him a "chile counter" because he was stingy and warned all her customers not to get too friendly with him. "Say hello to him and already he's eating your supper," she told them.

His perpetual gloom irritated her too. His long mournful face made her scowl. "He looks like a man dying without owing money," she said.

Oddly enough this sad man's best friend was Fausto Cárdenas, a jolly roasting ear vendor who smoked marijuana when he wasn't hawking his wares. Don Fausto came to the Flowers of Tepeyac every day puffing contentedly on one of the big marijuana cigarettes that Mexicans call *chonchomones*. His cigarettes smelled good, like burning tortillas, and smoking them made him happy and eloquent.

"La Juanita makes him happy as a buzzard drunk on sacred wine," Doña Lola told Pug Nose and me. When marijuana smoke thickened around his tousled head, he smilingly invited everyone to try *la yesca* so they could get as happy as he was. In these expansive moods he talked to his cigarette, gazing at it tenderly while he thanked it for making him dream dreams of the happy gypsies. Pug Nose and I liked to listen to him.

"Liberating herb, you're the father of death because you free me from the body's tyranny," he told the cigarette in sublime gratitude, oblivious to laughing countrymen.

Lupe Lara, owner of the Jarocho Barber Shop, ate there too. Don Lupe, small and sickly, with a pale twitching face, came to the food stand with a retired picador who sold lottery tickets. The two of them always livened things up.

After ordering pambazo, Don Lupe had the mariachis sing Veracruz songs filled with moonlight and languorous winds. Then he and the picador started arguing about bullfights. Countrymen crowded around to hear them debate on humanization of the fiesta. Don Lupe was against this. "It comes at a barbarous time in the world's history," he explained.

But the picador, old and partly blind, upheld it. "Caramba, the old public wanted horrors," he said, shuddering.

The barber's malicious brown eyes, tiny as huizache seeds, gleamed with savage enthusiasm every time he recalled matadors like Luis Freg and Rodolfo Gaona.

"They were men, not vedettes," he shouted. "And they fought Señor Toros with whiskers and flies on their muzzles—not indecent goats unworthy of Mexican plazas." He called Luis Freg "Don Valor" and referred to Rodolfo Gaona as the "Unforgettable Indian." He thanked God and the Celestial Court for letting him see them both on their most inspired afternoons. "I thank the dark virgin with the benign look for letting me see our great Indian of Guanajuato the day he smiled ironically at the fierce bull 'Butterfly' like Anatole France contemplating humanity," he said gratefully.

Silent as falling snow, the kindly old picador listened attentively while the spindly barber declaimed. But he didn't agree that old times were the best. He thought putting mattresses on horses' bellies was a good thing for the fiesta. "The modern methods of torture are much more humane," he said quietly. "Bulls used to open horses' bellies like bottles of wine." He never thought of the past with nostalgia. He was happier away from the bullring. "I'll never make their humps bleed again," he said without a trace of regret. "I'm happier selling lottery tickets."

Pug Nose and I listened to these debates. When they talked we could see mighty bulls big as cathedrals charging into pink and yellow capes that seemed to lift them to the skies.

An energetic old beggar, nicknamed the "Nightingale" because of his hacking cough, trapped our attention too. He came to the food stand every day with a red sweat rag around his neck and a ragged blanket filled with foxtail burrs and sand on his shoulder. He asked Doña Lola for menudo. "I haven't slept in a bed since Christ left Guanajuato and I'm dough-short and hungry," he told her. Doña Lola always gave him menudo. The Nightingale kept busy while he ate it. When countrymen with toothpicks in their mouths went by, he signaled them without getting up. "Paisa', I see you got yours," he remarked pleasantly. "Now how about giving an old man enough for a lump?" While the paisano dipped into his pocket, the Nightingale looked for

other toothpick-chewing countrymen. "Hey there, wait a min-
ute," he shouted when he saw them. He smiled when he took
their money.

"It's like the Alameda in Mexico City," he told Doña Lola.
"A man can sit on a bench and bing them going both ways
there."

He hunched over his menudo bowl, eating the tripe and
hominy slowly.

"I can't chew but I've got a good swallow," he explained.
He liked crying-sized onions even better than menudo. Doña
Lola always gave him one. He held it in a gnarled hand hard as
an August apple and bit into it greedily.

But the prizefighter Babe Zamarripa, nicknamed the "Tiger
of Juan de Dios," was more dynamic than any of them. Young
girls wore Sunday shawls and matrons their best house aprons
when the Baby came home after fighting in Mexico City. To the
Street of Crazy Women he always headed, looking handsome and
strong in a midnight blue suit and vividly striped shirt with his
healthy black hair slicked back in a glistening pompadour. The
Baby always looked happy. It was as though sunlight glowed
inside him and pushed out for release in smiles. He was always
glad to get back home. He showed it by shaking hands with every
man he saw and whacking all the women where the back changes
its name. He radiated confidence. When paisanos asked him if he
could beat lightweight champion Juan Zurita, he held his fists up
and smiled. *"Hijolé,* I'll knock that Guadalajara Express up in the
three-peso seats," he said, laughing. "That tapatio wouldn't
know which way to fall."

The Baby's good humor was contagious. He walked the
long street leaving laughter and black and blue hips in his wake.
Good looking or homely, it didn't matter. He whacked every
woman he saw. No one seemed to mind. Even dour women vendors with hair on their chins giggled girlishly. Beggar women
milled around him. Children did too. The Baby befriended them
all. Once he took Pug Nose and me to a carriage-trade cafe with
"English Spoken" on the door. Its opulence awed us so much
that we only picked at our food. Our mothers rebuked him, say-

ing he would spoil us.

"Such fine places aren't for our boys," they told him.

At one end of the street cheap dresses and aprons hung on hangers. Brown-skinned women with black hair wisping over their temples clustered there, looking at the clothes with rapt faces. They came from the poor neighborhoods fringing the bleak hills and stony gorges. The Baby flattered them all. He made them forget the dresses they wanted so much. Planting himself before them, he smiled at them admiringly. "Ay Señoras, in this world cats can look at queens," he said gallantly.

This made the poor paisanas beam. "Ay Baby, they may stretch the rope but they'll never hang you," they giggled.

Doña Lola pretended that she feared the Baby's advances. "I say the Lord's Prayer and the Apostles' Creed every time Andrés Zamarripa walks these streets of God," she said solemnly. But she giggled as much as the others and rubbed her hips just like they did after the Baby went by.

The Baby's accounts of his fights with Tobe de la Rosa and the Ranchero Ruiz held Pug Nose and me spellbound. One day we were listening to him tell how he outpointed Pachuca Kid Joe when Sister Guadalajara came looking for us.

Our teacher was a girlish-looking young nun, plump and pretty, with clear skin the color of coffee with a little cream in it. Usually she was smiling, but that day she wasn't. She walked toward the Flowers of Tepeyac with sinister certainty that she would find us there. Walking with her was Sister María de Jesús, a dour, middle-aged nun nicknamed "Sister Stiff Elbow" because she came from Monterrey, where people are popularly believed to be the stingiest in all Mexico.

Pug Nose saw them first. "Let's go, Amadito," he said.

But when I started to get up, the Baby put his hand on my shoulder and pressed me back firmly. He winked at Doña Lola and told us both not to run and keep calm. Then he called a mariachi over and began whispering to him. The mariachi nodded, grinning.

Pug Nose and I watched them uncertainly. The two Sisters of Charity were coming closer and closer. But the Baby didn't look worried at all. He smiled at the mariachi. "Sing *La Negra*,

José," he told him.

Strumming the bass strings of his Ramirez guitar, the mariachi waited until the two nuns got within earshot. When they did he threw back his head and began singing *La Negra* at the top of his lungs. He sang so loudly he made Sister Maria de Jesús clap her hands to her ears. But Sister Guadalajara didn't put her hands over her ears. She squared her shoulders and shouted: "Ay Jalisco, no te rajes" instead. We had heard many shouts, mostly *Ay Chihuahuas!* on the Street of the Crazy Women and these we were used to. But never before had we heard an Ay Jalisco! as clear and piercing as that one. Tears dribbled down Sister Guadalajara's cheeks as she sang with the mariachi. "Yo soy de meritito Jalisco!" she shouted in a voice quivering with emotion. Afterward she put her fingertips to her lips as though startled by her own shouts. But when Doña Lola and the Baby smiled at her, she began smiling too. Then she stood looking at the mariachi as though she wanted to hear him sing *La Negra* again, but couldn't get up enough nerve to ask him. He sang it again anyway.

This time Sister Guadalajara didn't sing or shout. She just stood there listening with big tears rolling down her cheeks. She smiled through her tears after he finished singing. "May the dark virgin protect you and cover you with her mantle," she whispered.

"Ay Sister, how you sang it," the Baby said with admiration. "Just to think of it makes my whiskers grow."

Sister Guadalajara beamed at him proudly. Then she looked at Pug Nose and me. We expected a scolding, but it didn't come. She blushed and smiled shyly instead.

It was Sister María de Jesús who finally spoke to us. She was smiling too. We could never remember seeing her smile before.

"Boys," she said softly. "Please don't tell the rest of the children how Sister Caridad shouted."

Pug Nose and I nodded and swore that we wouldn't. We never did. After that we played hooky as much as ever. But Sister Guadalajara, under the street's spell herself, never put burro's ears on us again.

GOING TO MARKET

My grandmother María de Jesús Avitia was the only one in my family who never got mad when I played hooky from Our Lady of the Thunderbolt School in Parral, Chihuahua.

My hooky playing didn't worry my grandmother at all. This was probably because she was born in the days when only rich Mexicans got much schooling.

"No one in your family was ever born in elegant diapers," she told me. "I myself never even learned to read and write, but I've been the happiest woman in all Mexico with your grandfather these many years."

She was a short, buxom woman, always smiling and cheerful. Heat circles from the charcoal-burning stove she cooked on always underscored her dark eyes. Gentle and soft-spoken, she never rebuked me as other older people did. Only when I shouted did she chide me and then always mildly.

"To loud talkers are born harelipped children," she reminded me then.

My grandmother was born in Delicias, a small Chihuahua cotton town, where her widowed father Antonio Lara worked as a street vendor. Many times she told me about him. From her I learned that he sold roasting ears in the fall, sweet potatoes after the first freeze, and oranges and sugar cane during the rest of the year.

"May the dark virgin protect him and cover him with her mantle," she said every time that she mentioned him.

But she advised me not to be a street vendor.

"Ay María madre mia, it's a hard life," she sighed. "You've got to walk, stop, and bawl all day long."

Only once in her life had my grandmother been out of Chihuahua. That was when my great-grandfather took her to Torreon, Coahuila, to visit her aunt. Her girlhood impressions of that colorful desert city, so different from Chihuahua, remained vivid. She never tired of telling me how refined Torreon's people were.

"Ay son, in Torreon the people like quality songs—boleros, tangos, and the like—and they never shout when they hear them," she told me. "But here in Chihuahua it's songs about bullets and knife thrusts that our people like best and everyone bawls with the singers."

I was a skinny boy with teeth missing out of the front of my mouth in those days. But my grandmother never stopped telling me how handsome I was. She was proud of my manners too. "Ay hija, my grandson opened the doors for me like a taxi driver," she told my mother proudly every time we came home from the Ignacio Allende market together.

These trips to the Allende market were always exciting for me. But I liked going to market best in the late fall. My grandmother did too. November's wild, windy days made us both too restless to stay indoors. So instead of going to school, I went to my grandmother's house and invited her to go to market. She always did.

"Ay madre, they won't wear shirt sleeves in Zacatecas today," she exclaimed when I came to her house on cold mornings.

Parral had many markets in those days. But I liked the Allende best. My grandmother did too even though she complained that it was noisier than King Solomon's wives. But it was colorful too. Going there was an event for us both.

Ordinarily my grandmother didn't dress up much in cold weather. She waddled around wearing a Santa Maria rebozo under a big Guaymeno sombrero and a ragged pair of workman's pants under her voluminous skirts.

But on market days she always put on her best percale dress and a black straw hat with two plaster cherries on it as well. Around her temple she wrapped a turkey-red bandana to protect her eyes from the cold.

Going to market put us both in good humor. We hurried down steep streets feeling rich enough to buy Fords. My grandmother walked with her arms folded across her bosom, gripping her elbows with both hands while I carried her oilcloth shopping bag.

We walked fast because we were both anxious to see everything that was done and hear everything that was said in the market's bright, cornucopia world on the Street of the Blind Singers. Walking fast, almost jogging, and shouting above the wind, she was more like a good friend playing hooky with me than a grandmother.

Jostling crowds always jammed the unpaved market street. Noise and confusion awaited us. Above vendor's hallelujah shouts rose the voices of the blind singers. They sat on camp chairs strumming battered guitars or guitarrones. Between songs they drywashed their chilled hands over tubs of burning wood set on brickbats.

Laughter rose from the rutted street's squalor. Bearded men in thready jumpers threw their heads back and shouted while the blind men sang of miracles and epic deeds. Meek women, shabby and careworn, became gay for a moment while street clowns played leapfrog and fire-eaters imitated volcanoes.

We picked our way through the crowds. Getting to the main market building took time. But once inside my grandmother bustled from stall to stall examining fruits and vegetables minutely. She was a careful shopper. Necessity made her so. She made the butcher cut all the fat off the meat before weighing it. She made sure she got the hardest bananas. The canny market vendors were her enemies. She never let them get the best of her. When they called on God and the Padre Hidalgo to bear witness that their balance scales gave good measure, she remained unimpressed.

"If you love God so much why don't you keep His commandments?" she asked them. Outside the market building was a plexus of outdoor food stands built of light boards, boxes, and tin sheeting. At these stands, stolid women with dust rags on their heads stirred fires with rush fans and tended smoke-blackened pots. I liked these food stands best of all. Their chile was hot enough to make a marble statue cry. Besides that they served the corn cakes called Maria Gordas that fell in the belly like a choir of angels.

To Mi Conchita food stand we always went after the marketing was done. Always smoky and reeking of pine pitch, this food stand was run by Doña Concepcion Contreras, a brawny woman with a rough, grainy face, who wore a big linen cook's cap. Nicknamed "La Dientona" because of her big teeth, she chain-smoked cornhusk cigarettes and swore like a mule skinner.

"Ay Doña Maria, you can't rout Demons with holy water and three Hail Marys," she explained every time my grandmother reproved her.

Moody and imperious, Doña Concha seldom tried to please her customers. The service at her stand wasn't good. When engrossed in gossip or arguments, she wouldn't wait on anyone until she had talked herself out. Then, too, she moved slowly because of her girth. Her elephantine dimensions made Chihuahuans say that she sat for two and ate for four. But her tamales stuffed with fiery chiles del arbol, were the bravest on the whole street. Poor workmen who put up a battle to earn a bean taco ate at her puesto. So did grizzled old Maderistas with tri-colored cockades on their jumpers.

Doña Concha's raucous arguments with her competitor Pancha la Jarocha attracted almost as many customers as her blazing tamales did. In a strident voice, keyed just under a shout, she called attention to the Jarocha's pretensions. This she did with caustic comments about the crayoned poster on her rival's food stand that read: "Sodas, Cervezas. You Welcome. English Spoken."

Doña Concha and the Jarocha reviled each other all day

long. Chattering like Tabasco parrots, they kept up a steady crossfire of abuse. Ragged men bunched around the food stands to hear them. I liked to listen to them while the champurrado was cooling.

Every time we went there, Doña Concha loudly asserted that the Jarocha accepted gifts from Cross-Eyed Emilio, a tomato vendor at the market. "How will Pancha pay for the dress he bought her—with smiles?" she asked her grinning onlookers.

"Ay Concha, not in front of the boy," my grandmother protested.

But the Jarocha, a spindly woman with a long plait of hair, shrugged these innuendoes aside.

"Much noise but nothing of opera," she gibed in her melodious Veracruz accent. "Lions don't frighten me, much less mice."

Mi Conchita was a nice place to be. On windy days when the market street smoked with arroyo sand, I liked to watch mariachi musicians with butterfly ties saw away at their violins. At Mi Conchita I ate steaming black beans with epazote while my grandmother chatted with Macario Meza, a blind guitar busker who sat at the stand all day long.

Don Macario was always glad to see my grandmother.

"May the blessed Santa Lucia guard your eyes, Doña Maria," he said after she greeted him.

The blind man was my grandmother's friend. She called him "my son" when she spoke to him. He was a rangy man, uncomplaining, polite, and so shy that countrymen nicknamed him the "Ranchero."

Handsome, strong, and good-natured, he liked to joke with my grandmother making her laugh with English words that he gleaned from tourists. When she asked him how he was feeling, his answer was always the same.

"Muy bad, Missus," he said, laughing loudly. "I no spick mucho English today."

Don Macario had a sweetheart before he was blinded in a Zacatecas mine explosion. He liked to tell my grandmother about her.

"Ay madre mia de la Conchita, she was lovelier than a
señorita from the capitol," he said warmly. "A girl for a king or a
great bullfighter—that I swear by the nails of the Cross. How
happy I was in the days when I thought of nothing but music,
payday, and that beautiful girl who promised to love me until it
rained in Sayula. But all that's a bead from another rosary now.
Some other bear's got the honey."

Don Macario played a seven-string guitar. I liked to watch
his broad fingers move over the strings, especially when he played
the Corrido of Alonzo who went to Texas. He sang and played
all day long. When he wasn't playing his guitar, he ran octaves on
a mouth organ. He had a fine, strong singing voice too. His songs
softened men with tempers like the thousand Demons.

Some broke down and cried when he sang the Corrido of
Benjamin Argumedo. Others squared their shoulders and howled
when he sang about Rosillo, the Sinaloa racehorse that poor
Mexicans bet their cows and pigs on. Then, too, he composed
corridos himself. He sold these songs on the street.

Hearing him sing Mexico's brave songs made me dream of
doing brave things too. I wanted to be a great boxer like Alberto
"Baby" Arizmendi, a heroic train engineer like Jesús Garcia, or
a Mexican Robin Hood like Heraclio Bernal so he would write
mañanitas about me. I liked Don Macario just as much as my
grandmother did. I hated his sweetheart for leaving him.

This gentle man dreamed of saving enough money so he
could go to La Luz Hospital in Mexico City for an operation to
restore his sight.

"If God is served then someday I'll see the many children
and dogs in the homes of the poor once again," he told my grandmother hopefully.

But Don Macario never earned much. His shyness kept him
from haranguing crowds to sell his ballads. Besides that it pre-
vented him from setting fixed prices for his songs.

I never stayed at the food stand as long as my grandmother
did. After eating, I rushed out in the street to join the crowds
watching General Popo, the clown, and Green Chile, the fire-
eater. My grandmother let me watch them for an hour or more.

I watched them until I heard her shout. Then I knew it was almost time to go home. But my grandmother never shouted at me alone. She shouted at everyone. She stood up and bawled until crowds turned away from General Popo and rushed up to the food stand to see what the trouble was. I always rushed over too. Hearing my grandmother shout and watching her wave her arms was more fun than seeing a clown or fire-eater even.

My grandmother shouted to help the blind singer sell ballads. She believed that a bawling woman could attract bigger crowds than a man. She never had any trouble attracting a crowd. As soon as she shouted "Attention, señores and señoras," countrymen began milling around her. When she got their attention, she waved fistfuls of Don Macario's ballads, printed on broadsides, at them.

"Paisano, come and buy the ballad of the heroic mother Antonia Rodriguez who saved her children from the wolves," she shouted. "Buy the corridos that tell of brave men who never doubled their spines and valiant women who never held their arms out to be twisted."

When countrymen were slow about buying, my grandmother grimaced and moaned.

"Qué barbaridad, don't you like the tune of my song," she snapped petulantly. "Don't stand like meek bulls that won't charge. Come on and buy the corridos about devout husbands who never look at blondes from the other side of the river."

But when countrymen bought ballads, she beamed at them all. "That which God gives, San Pedro blesses," she said when she took their money. "Now we're all eating with Guadalajara butter."

My grandmother harangued the crowds for fifteen minutes or more. By the time she got through, men and women were usually forming lines in front of Mi Conchita waiting their turns to buy ballads. Only then did she move away. Breathless and flushed, she stood at a distance watching countrymen drop their coins into Don Macario's money box.

"Ay son, I'm tired as a proletarian neighborhood," she

told me after the shouting was over. "I haven't bawled so much since I sold roasting ears with my father."

We watched the crowds until the last ballad was sold. When business was slow, she frowned. "Ay pobrecito," she murmured. "How will he pay for his operation?"

But when business was good, she looked radiant. One day I remember especially. That was when Don Macario sold forty pesos worth of ballads. My grandmother, happy and excited as a girl, clapped her hands while coins clinked into the blind singer's money box.

Flushed with her success in attracting the crowds, she smiled and winked at me triumphantly.

"A good rooster can crow in any corral," she said proudly.

After that she went home to cook my grandfather's dinner.

MALA TORRES

Now my old friend Memo Torres, once nicknamed La Malita, is different. He wears a black suit and a black hat and a Roman collar whenever he appears in El Paso. He comes to El Paso once a year and that is the only time Salvador Zavala and I ever get to see him. He still calls Chava and I by our first names and jokes with us when we are on our lunch hour at the ice plant. But now we are always polite to him and wait until he has gone before we finish our stories about Mexico.

"Good afternoon, Padre Guillermo," the other icemen say to him.

"Good afternoon, Padre Guillermo," I say to him.

Chava and I were in Our Lady of the Thunderbolt Church in Parral, Chihuahua, the day Memo said his first mass and became different. The church was crowded with people, relatives and friends, but Memo did not make a mistake. Chava knew because he was once an altar boy. Memo and Chava used to serve mass together when they went to Our Lady of the Thunderbolt School.

That was long ago—before Memo took the holy orders. He was like us then. He lived in our neighborhood La Primavera, and his father worked in La Prieta mine like ours. We played La Viborita and the Burro and the Rayuela every day in the streets.

Memo Torres had big placid eyes and a round smooth face with freckles across his nose. He had a calm air which underlined his deep, slow voice, and his black hair was always combed flat

with every strand in place. Broad-shouldered and compact with
bulging biceps, he was stronger than any of us. When we went to
the General Rodrigo Quevedo Gym, he bench-pressed more
weight and punched the light bag faster than anyone. Skipping
rope, shadow boxing, and working on the body bag, he looked
so much like Carlos Malacara, the Chihuahua lightweight who
once beat Champion Juan Zurita, that countrymen called him La
Malita or Little Mala.

"The boy moves like the great Mala himself," they enthused. "He's muy Mexicanota."

Memo was a year older, and we all tried to be like him.
The boys in our neighborhood always let him be the leader. He
had an air of importance which appealed to us in a way that
more reasonable people had never done. We did everything he
said. When he told Chava and I to play hooky with him, we
carried out his order though our mothers called us vagos for it.
But Chava and I agreed a scolding was a small price to pay for a
footloose day with Memo Torres.

Memo could think of more reasons for playing hooky
than a country Mexican can for going to Chihuahua City. Memo
and Chava and I lived within tobacco-spitting distance of school.
But at least once a week we never got there. Memo led us down to
the Street of the Crazy Women instead. Wandering up and down
it was more fun than staying in a classroom.

"It's more educational too," Memo always insisted, and we
couldn't help but agree. What we saw and heard there we never
forgot. The classroom was different; what we heard there we
never remembered.

The street enthralled Memo so wasn't much to look at. It
was just another broken-down street in a mining town that had
many like it. But to Memo and Chava and me it was an exciting
change from our own neighborhood with its poor homes on
crooked streets that wound up hillsides.

Then, too, in those days the Street of the Crazy Women
was a village in itself, northern as the nopal. One Viva Villa was
worth four Viva Zapatas there, and its mariachis sang of Blondie

López instead of Gabino Berrera. Chihuahuenses said this long, dusty street held more poor Mexicans than jails do. Its sights and sounds made them all feel at home. Mesquite wood smoke fogged it. Bawling vendors filled it. Misty vapors from steaming cornmeal drifted down it. There, women vendors scrubbed griddles with maguey fiber brushes, and countrymen scrubbed their teeth with their fingers in primitive Mexican village style.

Toward sidehills matted with chaparral, mesquite, and gobernadora, stood adobe homes with blessed palms hanging over their doors to keep evil spirits and lightning away. Stumpy cottonwoods, misted with gray veils woven by caterpillars, leaned before them. On clear days, the gossiping housewives, whose doings gave the street its name, sat on rush-plaited chairs under the heavy-leafed trees where, wrapped in thick mantas woven by High Sierra Indians, they patched Tenancingo rebozos and Santa Maria prayer shawls in the sunshine.

Their conversations were famous. They talked mostly about their husbands. Some said they wished they had gone into the convent instead of getting married. Others disagreed. "Ay Madre, it's better to undress one-horned drunkards than dress plaster saints," they insisted. Sometimes we listened until they drove us away.

We liked the street vendor's crowing cries too. They merged into a boisterous tympany. It was like Memo said. There was always something to see, something to listen to on the Street of the Crazy Women.

At one end of the street, near Jesús Maria Alley, was a rabbit warren cluster of rickety puestos that slumped and sagged like miniature Towers of Pisa. Robust women with nicknames like Maria la Bandida, La Trompitas, and La Chata Micaela, operated these foodstands popularly called agachados because they are so lowslung.

When we got hungry, we went to the Pearls of Coyame puesto run by Petra Porras, a buxom, smiling woman nicknamed Petra la Pozolera. In this little hut, made of rough boards so badly painted the wood's natural color showed through, we were always welcome.

Petra the Pozole Vendor, gray-haired with a broad, plea-sant face, greeted us with a wide smile that showed the glittering gold fillings of her teeth.

"Mira no mas—pura raza," she said when she saw us. "Ay, Jesus me valga. What vagabonds faces you have."

Sometimes we helped her scrub with shuck brooms and a bucket of hot water and lye. Then, too, we carried water on shoulder yokes, emptied ash buckets, and brought ice cubes for tepache.

"Now we'll eat with the big spoon," Doña Petra promised after all the chores were done.

The Pozole Vendor worked a la Mexicana singing at the top of her lungs. While she cooked pozole in a big black cazuela, we listened to her sing corridos that exuded blood and gun-powder and watched Jesús Maria Alley's milling crowds.

Many of the men going past us trudged as if they were exhausted or sick, their bodies stooped as if bent by pain. Where they'd been and where they'd yet to go, we couldn't tell. But many hungry men, broken by suffering, came to the Pozolera's puesto. Some, so weary they spoke in a whisper, told her they lived on mesquites, quelites, and even sabandijas. She never turned them away.

"Money is only a means of capping hunger," she said when she served them. "Eat, and may San Francisco give you his most sacred blessing."

The Pozolera's dark eyes were steady with hope and cour-age, and to us she was beautiful as an angel of Puebla. Many times this kindly woman told us about the destitute men who came to her puesto.

"They are men for whom a day without work is a tragedy—Ay Madre, the wind blows colder on them," she said. "Most don't have enough flesh on them for an albondiga, and all have a hunger from here to Balleza. May Nuestro Señor give them all a good place in the sky con todo y zapatos."

After lunch, we camped on a grassy bank near the Guana-juato Bridge where the Parral River was brown and swift and deep with quicksands making little whirlpools on the surface. The river bank was a nice place to be. The sound of the wind in the cottonwoods was like a gentle rain, and doves teetered nimbly on the branches and opened and closed their wings. Beyond the stone bridge, Parral looked like a mirage city with its low-built homes and broad, quiet squares colored by stone-bordered flower beds.

We built a chunk fire on a patch of beaten, grassless earth, and then sat down on the ground with our backs against a big limestone rock. We talked of far-off places and read dog-eared copies of *El Ruedo* and *Box y Lucha* until the first stars appeared and were reflected in the quiet river.

When Memo wasn't poring over boxing and bullfighting magazines, he read poems by Juan de Dios Peza and Manuel Plaza. Their poems inspired him to write poetry too. One poem, about the San Jose Bakery, I remember especially. This was probably because Jacinto Turrieta, a spindly Southerner with a dark scowling face, owned the bakery.

Don Chinto Turrieta came from Michoacan and his high-pitched voice was pleasant with the slurred, lilting drawl of Mexico's big harp country. His way of speaking was like a song in our ears. But he was high-strung and when he got mad his breath came with heavy, rasping gasps.

I remember the day Memo printed his poem on the San Jose Bakery's front window. It was pale and windy with the chilled tang of approaching winter, but Memo was bareheaded and the sleeves of his home-sewn shirt were rolled high on his biceps. With the incontrovertible assurance that characterized him, he stepped up to the window and wrote boldly and legibly. When he finished printing with yellow chalk, he stood back and studied the poem which read:

> *El que puso este letrero*
> *No supo lo que ponia*
> *San Jose fue carpintero*
> *No tuvo panaderia.*

(The man who named this place didn't know what he was doing. Saint Joseph was a carpenter. He didn't have a bakery.)

Chava and I waited to see what would happen. We did not have to wait long. Soon grinning paisanos gathered to read the verses. Their laughter filled Noche Triste Street like fresh notes on a musical scale, bringing Don Chinto out to see what the trouble was.

" ¿Tengo monos?" he snapped petulantly when countrymen smiled at him.

Don Chinto wrinkled his brows together, and read the poem. Then anger made him double up his fists, and he glared darkly at Memo.

"Son of the bad sleep, I'll make tortillas out of your snout," he shouted. "By the barricades of Guerrero I swear I'll carve a Viva Mexico on your face."

But Memo, resoluted and composed, remained adamant.

"What I wrote is the truth as God lives," he maintained.

When Don Chinto's tantrum subsided, he rubbed out the poem and then was quiet again. But, not long after that, he changed the bakery's name to El Suriano.

Now Memo is different. He has taken the holy orders. He wears a black suit, and we don't joke with him any more.

"Good morning, Padre," I say to him now.

CHIHUAHUA CAPIROTADA

When I was a boy, I worked for a fritanga vendor nicknamed María la Bandida on Saturdays. I carried water, emptied ash buckets, and brought ice cubes to her puesto in Jesús María Alley.

María la Bandida, burly with a broad, bumpy face, was Jesús María Alley's bravest fighter. When the Bandida fought, she squared off with her fists high like Luisito Castillo, the hard-hitting "Ghost of La Merced," whose picture hung in her puesto.

"Fight like hombrotes," she challenged her rival vendors. "Not like women—biting and scratching."

Most vendors feared the Bandida. When I first went to work there, I did too.

"Dark-hipped Mexicanito, I'll play 'Cielito Lindo' on your ribs with my fists," she threatened when I ran off to play Mama Leche.

But one day a ragged man, broken by suffering, came to the Bandida's puesto. He fingered his soyate sombrero nervously and looked down the alley furtively. Then he spoke so softly that I couldn't hear what he said. María la Bandida nodded.

"It don't matter—eat," she insisted. "You'll pay me another day."

After that I was never afraid of her.

* * *

A kindly old beggar, nicknamed Pancho Barbas because of his scrubby beard, waved to me on my way to school every morning. "Con Dios, muchachito," he shouted.

One morning Don Pancho asked me if my third-grade lessons were hard. When I said they were, he told me not to bother learning about the Sad Night or where Hidalgo was born or why Guerrero was executed.

"Laugh and play while you can, Chatito," he advised me. "Soon you'll be old enough to want an Adelita or a Valentina to do your cooking. Then you'll find out that picks and shovels aren't caramels."

*   *   *

My grandfather Trinidad Avitia managed to make a living singing and playing his Ramirez guitar. On Sunday mornings he would take me with him when he sang at the Hidalgo Market.

One of the most enthusiastic of his many admirers was a robust, middle-aged woman who ran the "Divine Strawberry" stand. This was Doña Guadalupe Carmona, nicknamed Lupe la Generala because of her fondness for recalling the days when she fought for General Francisco Villa.

Lupe the General wasn't one of those women who pray to San Antonio for sweethearts. When my grandfather sang romantic songs like "Maria Bonita" for other market vendors, she always begged him to stop. "Ay Mama Carlota, not that one Don Trini," she moaned. "Sing the brave one about how the Federals chased Benito Canales instead."

The songs she liked best were revolutionary ballads like "The Wet Buzzard" and "The Three Bald-Headed Women." But she liked corridos about manhunts, gunfights, and executions almost as well.

My grandfather's brave songs made the General wail and shout. They made her bawl: "Ay Chihuahua, land of brave men where nobody gets shot in the back."

Sometimes they even made her weep with fierce pride in

Panfilo Natera, Felipe Angeles, and other revolutionary heroes.

Once I asked my grandfather why Lupe the General always shouted and cried when he sang. I hadn't been a Mexican very long when I asked this for I was then not quite eight years old. My grandfather, a veteran observer of our countrymen, smiled at me.

"Every Chihuahuan kills fleas in his own way," he explained.

* * *

My grandmother María de Jesús Avitia liked Mexican music just as much as my grandfather did. She was a cheery, smiling woman, always laughing and joking with everyone. But sometimes she, too, lost her temper.

"I like everyone who walks on these streets of God," she often said with pride in her good nature. But after she said this, she bit her lip and added "except American blondies."

My grandmother showed her dislike for blondes every time American women asked my grandfather to sing "Cielito Lindo" for them on their sightseeing trips to Parral. He always did. But these street serenades made my grandmother so mad she wouldn't let him in the house.

"This home is for Christians," she shouted when my grandfather knocked at the door. "It's not for shameless old flirts who serenade American blondies instead of being content with what our own nation produces."

* * *

La Prieta mine shut down when I was seven years old and my father was out of work for three months.

My father couldn't afford to take me to the Azteca Theater on Sundays. So he would take me to Francisco I. Madero Street to hear roasting-ear vendors harangue the bullfight crowds instead.

Concepcion Lara, a short, stocky man with a roughly weathered face, was the vendor who shouted the loudest.

"Olé, for the fiesta of the thousand marvels," he bawled.

"May you see consecrated bulls that charge like saints and matadores who don't mind dying."

Madero Street was so narrow and crowded that taxicabs
couldn't go down it. Even the matadores had to walk to the
bullring. Chon Lara always wished them good luck.

"Go and fight happy bulls who know nothing of intrigues
and haven't read Machiavelli," he shouted. "And remember if
you die, your fame lives."

When Armillita, the famous Maestro of Saltillo, fought,
Chon Lara rushed up and shook hands with him.

"Don Fermin, may you draw honest bulls without com-
plexes or bad ideas," he said.

"I hope that God hears you," the Maestro of Saltillo
replied.

* * *

Another roasting-ear vendor nicknamed El Chilango never
missed a chance to praise fighting bulls when affluent bull
breeders went by.

"Olé, for the noble animals who never stoop to buffoon-
ery," he bawled. "Paisanos, you'll never see bulls make themselves
ridiculous by jumping over barrels like lions do when the crack of
a trainer's whip shocks them."

When bullfight crowds were small, the Chilango derided
countrymen who stayed home. "They think they're Mexicans
because they eat carnitas, drink sotol and tepache, and dance
the Jarabe Tapatio," he muttered glumly. "As for me I come
from Mexico City's Peralvillo quarter where everyone knows a
liter of pulque is more nourishing than a hundred Toluca chori-
zos, and a Sunday without bulls is unthinkable."

* * *

At María la Bandida's puesto, I made friends with a grizzled
old Maderista nicknamed Pancho Pistolas because he talked

about Pancho Villa so much. A beggar, he sat under the high arched doors of Our Lady of Guadalupe Church all day.

Eating pastries was Don Pancho's greatest pleasure. Just after dusk he would go to the Beautiful Indian Bakery to pick out two tarts crowned with whipped cream. He made his choices carefully, holding the tarts to the light so he could examine them minutely. Then he went to the Bandida's puesto to eat them with vanilla atole.

Pastries put him in expansive moods. Once he gave me fifty centavos after eating two of the tarts that Mexicans call Protestantes.

"Son, I wasn't born with my fists closed," he said when he gave me the coin. "Take it and buy yourself a new cap so some Maria will admire you."

*   *   *

One day I backed out of a fight with Tacho Mendoza, a classmate at Our Lady of the Thunderbolt School.

A crowd of boys had converged in the school courtyard in hopes of seeing a battle and they were all disappointed. They made so much noise that Father Estrada, the church pastor, came running out of the rectory. When Father Estrada found out what the trouble was, he called me over to one side.

"Be saintly, Muro, only not too much so," he told me. "If you're too saintly, your brothers will grind you into pinole."

After that I went back and fought Tacho.

CECILIA ROSAS

When I was in the ninth grade at Bowie High School in El Paso, I got a job hanging up women's coats at La Feria Department Store on Saturdays. It wasn't the kind of a job that had much appeal for a Mexican boy or for boys of any other nationality either. But the work wasn't hard, only boring. Wearing a smock, I stood around the Ladies' Wear Department all day long waiting for women customers to finish trying on coats so I could hang them up.

Having to wear a smock was worse than the work itself. It was an agonizing ordeal. To me it was a loathsome stigma of unmanly toil that made an already degrading job even more so. The work itself I looked on as onerous and effeminate for a boy from a family of miners, shepherds, and ditchdiggers. But working in Ladies' Wear had two compensations: earning three dollars every Saturday was one; being close to the Señorita Cecilia Rosas was the other.

This alluring young woman, the most beautiful I had ever seen, more than made up for my mollycoddle labor and the smock that symbolized it. My chances of looking at her were almost limitless. And like a good Mexican, I made the most of them. But I was only too painfully aware that I wasn't the only one who thought this saleslady gorgeous.

La Feria had water fountains on every one of its eight floors. But men liked best the one on the floor where Miss Rosas worked. So they made special trips to Ladies' Wear all day long to drink water and look at her.

Since I was only fourteen and in love for the first time, I looked at her more chastely than most. The way her romantic lashes fringed her obsidian eyes was especially enthralling to me. Then, too, I never tired of admiring her shining raven hair, her Cupid's-bow lips, the warmth of her gleaming white smile. Her rich olive skin was almost as dark as mine. Sometimes she wore a San Juan rose in her hair. When she did, she looked so very lovely I forgot all about what La Feria was paying me to do and stood gaping at her instead. My admiration was decorous but complete. I admired her hourglass figure as well as her wonderfully radiant face.

Other men admired her too. They inspected her from the water fountain. Some stared at her boldly, watching her trimly rhythmic hips sway. Others, less frank and open, gazed furtively at her swelling bosom or her shapely calves. Their effrontery made me indignant. I, too, looked at these details of Miss Rosas. But I prided myself on doing so more romantically, far more poetically than they did, with much more love than desire.

Then, too, Miss Rosas was the friendliest as well as the most beautiful saleslady in Ladies' Wear. But the other salesladies, Mexican girls all, didn't like her. She was so nice to them all they were hard put to justify their dislike. They couldn't very well admit they disliked her because she was pretty. So they all said she was haughty and imperious. Their claim was partly true. Her beauty was Miss Rosas' only obvious vanity. But she had still another. She prided herself on being more American than Mexican because she was born in El Paso. And she did her best to act, dress, and talk the way Americans do. She hated to speak Spanish, disliked her Mexican name. She called herself Cecile Roses instead of Cecilia Rosas. This made the other salesladies smile derisively. They called her La Americana or the Gringa from Xochimilco every time they mentioned her name.

Looking at this beautiful girl was more important than money to me. It was my greatest compensation for doing work that I hated. She was so lovely that a glance at her sweetly ex-

pressive face was enough to make me forget my shame at wearing a smock and my dislike for my job with its eternal waiting
around.

Miss Rosas was an exemplary saleslady. She could be fri-
volous, serious or demure, primly efficient too, molding herself
to each customer's personality. Her voice matched her exotically
mysterious eyes. It was the richest, the softest I had ever heard.
Her husky whisper, gentle as a rain breeze, was like a tender
caress. Hearing it made me want to dream and I did. Romantic
thoughts burgeoned up in my mind like rosy billows of hope
scented with Miss Rosas' perfume. These thoughts made me so
languid at my work that the floor manager, Joe Apple, warned
me to show some enthusiasm for it or else suffer the conse-
quences.

But my dreams sapped my will to struggle, making me
oblivious to admonitions. I had neither the desire nor the energy
to respond to Joe Apple's warnings. Looking at Miss Rosas used
up so much of my energy that I had little left for my work. Miss
Rosas was twenty, much too old for me, everyone said. But what
everyone said didn't matter. So I soldiered on the job and watched her, entranced by her beauty, her grace. While I watched I
dreamed of being a hero. It hurt me to have her see me doing
menial work. But there was no escape from it. I needed the job
to stay in school. So more and more I took refuge in dreams.

When I had watched her as much, if not more, than I
could safely do without attracting the attention of other alert
Mexican salesladies, I slipped out of Ladies' Wear and walked up
the stairs to the top floor. There I sat on a window ledge smoking
Faro cigarettes, looking down at the city's canyons, and best of
all, thinking about Miss Rosas and myself.

They say Chihuahua Mexicans are good at dreaming because the mountains are so gigantic and the horizons so vast in
Mexico's biggest state that men don't think pygmy thoughts
there. I was no exception. Lolling on the ledge, I became what
I wanted to be. And what I wanted to be was a handsome American Miss Rosas could love and marry. The dreams I dreamed

were imaginative masterpieces, or so I thought. They transcended
the insipid realities of a casual relationship, making it vibrantly
thrilling and infinitely more romantic. They transformed me
from a colorless Mexican boy who put women's coats away into
the debonair American, handsome, dashing and worldly, that I
longed to be for her sake. For the first time in my life I revelled
in the magic of fantasy. It brought happiness. Reality didn't.

But my window ledge reveries left me bewildered and
shaken. They had a narcotic quality. The more thrillingly romantic fantasies I created, the more I needed to create. It got so I
couldn't get enough dreaming time in Ladies' Wear. My kind of
dreaming demanded disciplined concentration. And there was
just too much hubbub, too much gossiping, too many coats to
be put away there.

So I spent less time in Ladies' Wear. My flights to the window ledge became more recklessly frequent. Sometimes I got
tired sitting there. When I did, I took the freight elevator down
to the street floor and brazenly walked out of the store without
so much as punching a time clock. Walking the streets quickened
my imagination, gave form and color to my thoughts. It made
my brain glow with impossible hopes that seemed incredibly
easy to realize. So absorbed was I in thoughts of Miss Rosas and
myself that I bumped into Americans, apologizing mechanically
in Spanish instead of English, and wandered down South El Paso
Street like a somnambulist, without really seeing its street vendors, cafes and arcades, tattoo shops, and shooting galleries
at all.

But if there was confusion in these walks there was some
serenity too. Something good did come from the dreams that
prompted them. I found I could tramp the streets with a newly
won tranquillity, no longer troubled by, or even aware of, girls
in tight skirts, overflowing blouses, and drop-stitch stockings.
My love for Miss Rosas was my shield against the furtive thoughts
and indiscriminate desires that had made me so uneasy for a
year or more before I met her.

Then, too, because of her, I no longer looked at the pictures of voluptuous women in the *Vea* and *Vodevil* magazines

at Zamora's newsstand. The piquant thoughts Mexicans call
malos deseos were gone from my mind. I no longer thought
about women as I did before I fell in love with Miss Rosas.
Instead, I thought about a woman, only one. This clear-cut ob-
jective and the serenity that went with it made me understand
something of one of the nicest things about love.

I treasured the walks, the window-ledge sittings, and the
dreams that I had then. I clung to them just as long as I could.
Drab realities closed in on me chokingly just as soon as I gave
them up. My future was a time clock with an American Mister
telling me what to do and this I knew only too well. A career as
an ice-dock laborer stretched ahead of me. Better said, it dangled
over me like a Veracruz machete. My uncle Rodolfo Avitia, a
straw boss on the ice docks, was already training me for it. Every
night he took me to the mile-long docks overhanging the Southern Pacific freight yards. There he handed me tongs and made
me practice tripping three-hundred-pound ice blocks so I could
learn how to unload an entire boxcar of ice blocks myself.

Thinking of this bleak future drove me back into my
fantasies, made me want to prolong them forever. My imagination was taxed to the breaking point by the heavy strain I put
on it.

I thought about every word Miss Rosas had ever said to
me, making myself believe she looked at me with unmistakable
tenderness when she said them. When she said: "Amado, please
hang up this fur coat," I found special meaning in her tone. It
was as though she had said: "Amadito, I love you."

When she gave these orders, I pushed into action like a
man blazing with a desire to perform epically herioc feats. At
such times I felt capable of putting away not one but a thous-
and fur coats, and would have done so joyously.

Sometimes on the street I caught myself murmuring:
"Cecilia, *linda amorcita,* I love you." When these surges swept
over me, I walked down empty streets so I could whisper:
"Cecilia, *te quiero con toda mi alma*" as much as I wanted to and
mumble everything else that I felt. And so I emptied my heart on
the streets and window ledge while women's coats piled up in
Ladies' Wear.

But my absences didn't go unnoticed. Once an executive-looking man, portly, gray, and efficiently brusque, confronted me while I sat on the window ledge with a Faro cigarette pasted to my lips, a cloud of tobacco smoke hanging over my head, and many perfumed dreams inside it. He had a no-nonsense approach that jibed with his austere mien. He asked me what my name was, jotted down my work number, and went off to make a report on what he called "sordid malingering."

Other reports followed this. Gruff warnings, stern admonitions, and blustery tirades developed from them. They came from both major and minor executives. These I was already inured to. They didn't matter anyway. My condition was far too advanced, already much too complex to be cleared up by mere lectures, fatherly or otherwise. All the threats and rebukes in the world couldn't have made me give up my window-ledge reveries or kept me from roaming city streets with Cecilia Rosas' name on my lips like a prayer.

The reports merely made me more cunning, more doggedly determined to city-slick La Feria out of work hours I owed it. The net result was that I timed my absences more precisely and contrived better lies to explain them. Sometimes I went to the men's room and looked at myself in the mirror for as long as ten minutes at a time. Such self-studies filled me with gloom. The mirror reflected an ordinary Mexican face, more homely than comely. Only my hair gave me hope. It was thick and wavy, deserving a better face to go with it. So I did the best I could with what I had, and combed it over my temples in ringlets just like the poets back in my hometown of Parral, Chihuahua, used to do.

My inefficiency, my dreams, my general lassitude could have gone on indefinitely, it seemed. My life at the store wavered between bright hope and leaden despair, unrelieved by Miss Rosas' acceptance or rejection of me. Then one day something happened that almost made my overstrained heart stop beating.

It happened on the day Miss Rosas stood behind me while I put a fur coat away. Her heady perfume, the fragrance of her warm healthy body, made me feel faint. She was so close to me I thought about putting my hands around her lissome waist and hugging her as hard as I could. But thoughts of subsequent disgrace deterred me, so instead of hugging her I smiled wanly and asked her in Spanish how she was feeling.

"Amado, speak English," she told me. "And pronounce the words slowly and carefully so you won't sound like a country Mexican."

Then she looked at me in a way that made me the happiest employee who ever punched La Feria's time clock.

"Amadito," she whispered the way I had always dreamed she would.

"Yes, Señorita Cecilia," I said expectantly.

Her smile was warmly intimate. "Amadito, when are you going to take me to the movies?" she asked.

Other salesladies watched us, all smiling. They made me so nervous I couldn't answer.

"Amadito, you haven't answered me," Miss Rosas said teasingly. "Either you're bashful as a village sweetheart or else you don't like me at all."

In voluble Spanish, I quickly assured her the latter wasn't the case. I was just getting ready to say "Señorita Cecilia, I more than like you, I love you" when she frowned and told me to speak English. So I slowed down and tried to smooth out my ruffled thoughts.

"Señorita Cecilia," I said. "I'd love to take you to the movies any time."

Miss Rosas smiled and patted my cheek. "Will you buy me candy and popcorn?" she said.

I nodded, putting my hand against the imprint her warm palm had left on my face.

"And hold my hand?"

I said "yes" so enthusiastically it made her laugh. Other salesladies laughed too. Dazed and numb with happiness, I watched Miss Rosas walk away. How proud and confident she was, how wholesomely clean and feminine. Other salesladies were looking at me and laughing.

Miss Sandoval came over to me. *"Ay papacito,"* she said. "With women you're the divine tortilla."

Miss de la Rosa came over too. "When you take the Americana to the movies, remember not to speak Christian," she said. "And be sure you wear the pants that don't have any patches on them."

What they said made me blush and wonder how they knew what we had been talking about. Miss Arroyo came over to join them. So did Miss Torres.

"Amado, remember women are weak and men aren't made of sweet bread," Miss Arroyo said.

This embarrassed me but it wasn't altogether unpleasant. Miss Sandoval winked at Miss de la Rosa, then looked back at me.

"Don't go too fast with the Americana, Amado," she said. "Remember the procession is long and the candles are small."

They laughed and slapped me on the back. They all wanted to know when I was going to take Miss Rosas to the movies. "She didn't say," I blurted out without thinking.

This brought another burst of laughter. It drove me back up to the window ledge where I got out my package of Faros and thought about the wonderful thing that had happened. But I was too nervous to stay there. So I went to the men's room and looked at myself in the mirror again, wondering why Miss Rosas liked me so well. The mirror made it brutally clear that my looks hadn't influenced her. So it must have been something else, perhaps character. But that didn't seem likely either. Joe Apple had told me I didn't have much of that. And other store officials had bulwarked his opinion. Still, I had seen homely men walking the streets of El Paso's Little Chihuahua quarter with beautiful Mexican women and no one could explain that either. Anyway it was time for another walk. So I took one.

This time I trudged through Little Chihuahua, where both Miss Rosas and I lived. Little Chihuahua looked different to me that day. It was a broken-down Mexican quarter honeycombed with tenements, Mom and Pop groceries, herb shops, cafes, and spindly salt-cedar trees; with howling children running its streets and old Mexican revolutionaries sunning themselves on its curbs like iguanas. But on that clear frosty day it was the world's most romantic place because Cecilia Rosas lived there.

While walking, I reasoned that Miss Rosas might want to go dancing after the movies. So I went to Professor Toribio Ortega's dance studio and made arrangements to take my first lesson. Some neighborhood boys saw me when I came out. They bawled *"Mariquita"* and made flutteringly effeminate motions, all vulgar if not obscene. It didn't matter. On my lunch hour I went back and took my first lesson anyway. Professor Ortega danced with me. Softened by weeks of dreaming, I went limp in his arms imagining he was Miss Rosas.

The rest of the day was the same as many others before it. As usual I spent most of it stealing glances at Miss Rosas and slipping up to the window ledge. She looked busy, efficient, not like a woman in love. Her many other admirers trooped to the water fountain to look at the way her black silk dress fitted her curves. Their profane admiration made me scowl even more than I usually did at such times.

When the day's work was done, I plodded home from the store just as dreamily as I had gone to it. Since I had no one else to confide in, I invited my oldest sister, Dulce Nombre de María, to go to the movies with me. They were showing Jorge Negrete and Maria Felix in *El Rapto* at the Colon Theater. It was a romantic movie, just the kind I wanted to see.

After it was over, I bought Dulce Nombre *churros* and hot *champurrado* at the Golden Taco Cafe. And I told my sister all about what had happened to me. She looked at me thoughtfully, then combed my hair back with her fingertips as though trying to soothe me. "Manito," she said, softly. "I wouldn't. . . " Then she looked away and shrugged her shoulders.

On Monday I borrowed three dollars from my Uncle Rodolfo without telling him what it was for. Miss Rosas hadn't told me what night she wanted me to take her to the movies. But the way she had looked at me made me think that almost any night would do. So I decided on Friday. Waiting for it to come was hard. But I had to keep my mind occupied. So I went to

Zamora's news stand to get the Alma Nortena songbook. Pouring through it for the most romantic song I could find, I decided on *La Cecilia.*

All week long I practiced singing it on my way to school and in the shower after basketball practice with the Little Chihuahua Tigers at the Sagrado Corazón gym. But, except for singing this song, I tried not to speak Spanish at all. At home I made my mother mad by saying in English, "Please pass the sugar."

My mother looked at me as though she couldn't believe what she had heard. Since my Uncle Rodolfo couldn't say anything more than "hello" and "goodbye" in English, he couldn't tell what I had said. So my sister Consuelo did.

"May the Dark Virgin with the benign look make this boy well enough to speak Christian again," my mother whispered.

This I refused to do. I went on speaking English even though my mother and uncle didn't understand it. This shocked my sisters as well. When they asked me to explain my behavior, I parroted Miss Rosas, saying, "We're living in the United States now."

My rebellion against being a Mexican created an uproar. Such conduct was unorthodox, if not scandalous, in a neighborhood where names like Burgiaga, Rodriguez, and Castillo predominated. But it wasn't only the Spanish language that I lashed out against.

"Mother, why do we always have to eat *sopa, frijoles, refritos, mondongo,* and *pozole?*" I complained. "Can't we ever eat roast beef or ham and eggs like Americans do?"

My mother didn't speak to me for two days after that. My Uncle Rodolfo grimaced and mumbled something about renegade Mexicans who want to eat ham and eggs even though the Montes Packing Company turned out the best *chorizo* this side of Toluca. My sister Consuelo giggled and called me a Rio Grande Irishman, an American Mister, a gringo, and a *bolillo.* Dulce Nombre looked at me worriedly.

Life at home was almost intolerable. Cruel jokes and mocking laughter made it so. I moped around looking sad as a day without bread. My sister Consuelo suggested I go to the courthouse and change my name to Beloved Wall which is English for Amado Muro. My mother didn't agree. "If *Nuestro Señor* had meant for Amadito to be an American he would have given him a name like Smeeth or Jonesy," she said. My family was unsympathetic. With a family like mine, how could I ever hope to become an American and win Miss Rosas?

Friday came at last. I put on my only suit, slicked my hair down with liquid vaseline, and doused myself with Dulce Nombre's perfume.

"Amado's going to serenade that pretty girl everyone calls La Americana," my sister Consuelo told my mother and uncle when I sat down to eat. "Then he's going to take her to the movies."

This made my uncle laugh and my mother scowl.

"*Qué pantalones tiene* (what nerve that boy's got)," my uncle said, "to serenade a twenty-year-old woman."

"La Americana," my mother said derisively. "That one's Mexican as pulque cured with celery."

They made me so nervous I forgot to take off my cap when I sat down to eat.

"Amado, take off your cap," my mother said. "You're not in La Lagunilla Market."

My uncle frowned. "All this boy thinks about is kissing girls," he said gruffly.

"But my boy's never kissed one," my mother said proudly.

My sister Consuelo laughed. "That's because they won't let him," she said.

This wasn't true. But I couldn't say so in front of my mother. I had already kissed Emalina Uribe from Porfirio Díaz Street not once but twice. Both times I'd kissed her in a darkened doorway less than a block from her home. But the kisses were over so soon we hardly had time to enjoy them. This was because Ema was afraid of her big brother, the husky one nicknamed Toro, would see us. But if we'd had more time it would have been better, I knew.

Along about six o'clock the three musicians who called themselves the Mariachis of Tecalitlán came by and whistled for me, just as they had said they would. They never looked better than they did on that night. They had on black and silver charro uniforms and big, black, Zapata sombreros.

My mother shook her head when she saw them. "Son, who ever heard of serenading a girl at six o'clock in the evening," she said. "When your father had the mariachis sing for me it was always two o'clock in the morning—the only proper time for a six-song *gallo*."

But I got out my Ramirez guitar anyway. I put on my cap and rushed out to give the mariachis the money without even kissing my mother's hand or waiting for her to bless me. Then we headed for Miss Rosas' home. Some boys and girls I knew were out in the street. This made me uncomfortable. They looked at me wonderingly as I led the mariachi band to Miss Rosas' home.

A block away from Miss Rosas' home I could see her father, a grizzled veteran who fought for Pancho Villa, sitting on the curb reading the Juarez newspaper, *El Fronterizo*.

The sight of him made me slow down for a moment. But I got back in stride when I saw Miss Rosas herself.

She smiled and waved at me. "Hello, Amadito," she said.

"Hello, Señorita Cecilia," I said.

She looked at the mariachis, then back to me.

"Ay, Amado, you're going to serenade your girl," she said. I didn't reply right away. Then when I was getting ready to say "Señorita Cecilia, I came to serenade you," I saw the American man sitting in the sports roadster at the curb.

Miss Rosas turned to him. "I'll be right there, Johnny," she said.

She patted my cheek. "I've got to run now, Amado," she said. "Have a real nice time, darling."

I looked at her silken legs as she got into the car. Everything had happened so fast I was dazed. Broken dreams made my head spin. The contrast between myself and the poised

American in the sports roadster was so cruel it made me wince.

She was happy with him. That was obvious. She was smiling and laughing, looking forward to a good time. Why had she asked me to take her to the movies if she already had a boyfriend? Then I remembered how the other salesladies had laughed, how I had wondered why they were laughing when they couldn't even hear what we were saying. And I realized it had all been a joke, everyone had known it but me. Neither Miss Rosas nor the other salesladies had ever dreamed I would think she was serious about wanting me to take her to the movies.

The American and Miss Rosas drove off. Gloomy thoughts oppressed me. They made me want to cry. To get rid of them I thought of going to one of the "bad death" cantinas in Juárez where tequila starts fights and knives finish them—to one of the cantinas where the panders, whom Mexicans call *burros*, stand outside shouting "It's just like Paris, only not so many people" was where I wanted to go. There I could forget her in Jalisco-state style with mariachis, tequila, and night-life women. Then I remembered I was so young that night-life women would shun me and *cantineros* wouldn't serve me tequila.

So I thought some more. Emalina Uribe was the only other alternative. If we went over to Porfirio Díaz Street and serenaded her I could go back to being a Mexican again. She was just as Mexican as I was, Mexican as *chicharrones*. I thought about smiling, freckle-faced Ema.

Ema wasn't like the Americana at all. She wore wash dresses that fitted loosely and even ate the *melcocha* candies Mexicans liked so well on the street. On Sundays she wore a Zamora shawl to church and her mother wouldn't let her use lipstick or let her put on high heels.

But with a brother like Toro who didn't like me anyway, such a serenade might be more dangerous than romantic. Besides that, my faith in my looks, my character, or whatever it was that made women fall in love with men, was so undermined I could already picture her getting into a car with a handsome American just like Miss Rosas had done.

The Mariachis of Tecalitlan were getting impatient. They had been paid to sing six songs and they wanted to sing them. But they were all sympathetic. None of them laughed at me.

"Amado, don't look sad as I did the day I learned I'd never be a millionare," the mariachi captain said, putting his arm around me. "If not that girl, then another."

But without Miss Rosas there was no one we could sing *La Cecilia* to. The street seemed bleak and empty now that she was gone. And I didn't want to serenade Ema Uribe even though she hadn't been faithless as Miss Rosas had been. It was true she hadn't been faithless, but only lack of opportunity would keep her from getting into a car with an American, I reasoned cynically.

Just about then Miss Rosas' father looked up from his newspaper. He asked the mariachis if they knew how to sing *Cananea Jail*. They told him they did. Then they looked at me. I thought it over for a moment. Then I nodded and started strumming the bass strings of my guitar. What had happened made it only too plain I could never trust Miss Rosas again. So we serenaded her father instead.

SOLEDAD CASTILLO

Soledad Castillo was the wealthiest woman in Parral, Chihuahuas' aristocratic San Juan de Dios neighborhood.

The rents from the five homes and farm her widowed father had left her brought her more than five thousand pesos a month. But even though she had more than enough money to live on, Doña Chole wouldn't stop working.

She had never married. Nor did she have any desire to do so. She never went to Our Lady of Mercy Church at five o'clock in the morning to ask San Antonio to send her a husband as other Parral spinsters did. She was content to live by herself in a Moorish-style home with a bubbling fountain in front, tall willow trees at the sides, and a mud and mortar wall topped with broken glass surrounding it.

Doña Chole lived an exemplary life. Tequila and sotol she never touched. Smoking cornhusk cigarettes was her only vice. And she more than offset this with her industry.

"By working I eat and by eating I live," she told everyone. "One can never never have too much security."

She was a gaunt woman with an angular face the color of coffee with a little cream in it. Her lifeless gray hair straggled over her corrugated brows like shoestrings and half moons of pouchy flesh underscored her obsidian eyes. But she dressed modishly and powdered her seamy face until it was pale as clown white to try to keep the wrinkles from showing.

When neighborhood comadres asked her why she didn't

spend the summers in Cuernavaca like many of Parral's rich people did, the elderly spinster put her hands to her ears as though she had heard something immoral.

"Ay Señora Santa, trips to Cuerna' cost money," she said. "And I'm a poor woman who has to scratch her back with her own fingernails. Comadres, I swear by the nails of the cross that I have to walk by myself in this life for none of my countrymen want to carry me."

But when neighbors asked her what kind of work she did, she always changed the subject adroitly. Her evasiveness made them conclude she kept busy collecting rents and overseeing repairs on her properties. Doña Chole never said anything to make them think otherwise.

Her work week began after early mass on Sunday. At eight o'clock she left her luxurious home with a knapsack tucked under her arm. Then she walked down the Street of the Tree to the poverty-ridden Porfirio Parra neighborhood where she owned a crumbling adobe home she never rented. This home, bare inside and unheated, was set apart from others in the neighborhood by a row of stumpy cottonwood trees overhanging a rock-filled arroyo.

Doña Chole used it as a dressing room and storehouse for her many statues of saints. Before going into the house, she always looked up and down the street to make sure that no one was watching her.

Once inside, she opened her knapsack and took out her work clothes. She slipped out of her stylish dress and got into a ragged black skirt, a faded blue jumper, a carpenter's apron, and a pair of untanned prison brogans several sizes too big for her. After changing clothes she dusted off the Saints' statues with a tattered chamois. Then she covered her head with a blue rebozo and went outside with a statue of San Martin Caballero.

When Doña Chole walked out of the house she no longer looked or acted like a prosperous property owner. She became the ragged beggar woman nicknamed "La Santera" instead. Miners and housewives saw her tramping the unpaved streets of

Parral's proletarian neighborhoods every day. They called her "La Santera" because she always carried saints' statues.

Her dolorous expression and wasted body inspired pity in them all. They felt even more sorry for the Santera when they heard her quavery voice. She always spoke in a husked whisper as though she was too weak to beg alms in normal tones.

Doña Chole trudged past La Panchita grocery and La Sierra de Chihuahua cafe begging alms from everyone she saw. "The Virgencita will pay you," she whispered when Chihuahuans put coins in her hand.

She walked the rutted streets of poor neighborhoods where tousle-haired children put boards over oil drums so they could use them for seesaws. She walked past khaki-colored adobe homes, crumbling and ridged like soda crackers, where housewives stirred fires in charcoal burning stoves with rush fans and sleepy dogs sunned themselves in the doorways.

Sometimes she stopped at outdoor food stands with canvas flaps dangling down from their roofs like earmuffs. "May today find you with the pure sentiment of charity in your hearts," she told men and women eating there.

When they gave her money, she slipped the coins into the nail pockets of her carpenter's apron and smiled beatifically. "Good and Sainted days may you all have," she murmured. "And may the dark Virgin who spoke with Juan Diego answer all your prayers."

Everyone pitied the withered Santera. And many gave her money as she plodded along to Melchior Ocampo Street. Even barefooted newsboys who sat on Doblado Street curbs eating fritanga and mimicking street venders' cries gave her coins. But Doña Chole didn't depend on countrymen alone when she begged alms. She had learned enough English to beg from tourists besides. So she also stopped in opulent cafes with "English Spoken" on their doors.

She made so many stops at cafes and outdoor food stands it usually took her an hour or more to get to Melchior Ocampo Street with her statue of San Martin Caballero.

When she got there she carried the statue into smoke fogged cantinas where short card gamblers and domino hustlers kept games going night and day. She held the statue up so all the gamblers could see it. The costly statue, made by Pueblas' famous "santeros," never failed to impress everyone. Gamblers made the sign of the cross when they saw it. After they did, Doña Chole asked them for alms. And since San Martin Caballero is the patron saint of Mexico's gamblers they seldom, if ever, refused her.

There were so many cantinas and so many gamblers on Melchior Ocampo Street that it took Doña Chole almost two hours to canvass them all. But she worked them so thoroughly that the nail pockets of her carpenter's apron were always bulging with bills and coins by the time she got ready to take the statue back to her home in the Porfirio Parra neighborhood.

On Monday, Doña Chole got out her statue of the Good Thief San Dimas, patron saint of Mexico's lawbreakers. This she carried to the bad death hotels on Mariscal street where most of Parral's hoodlums lived. She showed the saint's statue to raffish pickpockets, burly jackrollers, ferrety procurers and cantina Tarzans. Then she asked them for alms. They always gave them.

Doña Chole comforted the sick in proletarian neighborhoods on Tuesday. She carried her statue of San Nicolas de Bari to their homes. She taught sick persons special prayers to this saint, the protector of Mexicans who are ill. She prayed with them before asking for alms. Sick Chihuahuans seldom refused her.

Doña Chole begged alms from Parral's many mariachis, wandering musicians, and street singers on Wednesday. On this day she went to Ignacio Allende Street, narrow and crowded as Guanajuato's Street of the Kiss. She carried her statue of Santa Cecilia, patroness of Mexico's musicians, with her. She begged alms from every musician in sight. The musicians were usually just as generous as the gamblers, thieves, and sick persons had been.

Doña Chole never worked on Thursday morning. She stayed home to do her washing and cleaning instead. But in the afternoon she was back on the street with a statue of Santa Rita de Casia, patroness of Mexico's housewives. She called on housewives all afternoon long. But instead of begging alms as she usually did, she sold them prayers printed on broadsides.

Doña Chole sold housewives' prayers to San Pedro, La Magnifica, and the Santo Angel de la Guardia. She took eggs, flour tortillas, gorditas, cinnamon, and milk in payment from housewives who didn't have money.

Then, too, on Thursday, Doña Chole also went to poor neighborhoods along the Parral river where floods often washed homes away. She carried a statue of San Severino, the anchorite saint who protects Mexicans against wild waters as well as malign winds and lung ailments. She begged alms and also sold special prayers to San Severino to residents of these low-lying areas.

On Friday morning, Doña Chole did her marketing instead of working. But before going down to the Hidalgo market, she stopped at the Jose Maria Morelos plaza where grizzled Madero revolution veterans talked about Pancho Villa and Maclovio Herrera all day long.

When the veterans saw her coming, they took fistfuls of the strong dark tobacco northern Mexicans call *macuchi* out of the brims of their Zoyate sombreros so they could put them into the pouch she held out every time she asked them for tobacco. Since the cornhusk cigarettes Doña Chole smoked were hard to keep burning, she asked them for matches as well. Then she went on to the market.

Vegetable and fruit merchants made the sign of the cross when they saw her. "Ay Maria madre mia, trying to deal with Doña Chole is like spitting in the sky and hoping it doesn't come back in your face," they all muttered.

She was the despair of these merchants because she haggled with them all. Sometimes they even kissed the pesos she spent in joy over having seen her money.

After she did her marketing, Doña Chole went back to work. But she didn't go out with saints' statues on Friday. She carried a knapsack filled with bottles of holy water instead.

These she sold to housewives for use in driving the Devil away. She swore such exorcisms were infallible. "Comadres, just rub the holy water on your knees and tell the Devil and all his chamucos to get out of the house," she told housewives.

On that day she also sold housewives prayers guaranteed to rid homes of evil spirits so Christians could sleep in peace.

But on cold Fridays when gnashing winds shucked through cottonwood lofts and rolled tumbleweeds down unpaved streets like hoops, Doña Chole didn't go from door to door.

Instead she looked at the calendar to see what Chihuahuans were celebrating their Saints' Days. Then she went to their homes to congratulate them. When they invited her to eat, she never refused.

"I'm just a poor beggar woman," she whispered. "But when it's time to eat we're all equal."

But after eating, she usually sold her hosts special prayers to the saints whose day they were born on.

Then, too, on cold afternoons, Doña Chole sometimes begged old clothes. "Ay how the poor suffer," she told housewives while she stood shivering with cold in their homes. "I pray San Martin will share his ragged cape with me tonight."

The housewives always responded. Some even gave her sarapes as well as old clothes. These Doña Chole sold to workmen from the High Sierra.

Saturday was always her busiest day as well as her most profitable. Sometimes she earned more money on that day than on all the others combined.

On Saturday she dusted off her statue of Mary Magdalena and carried it to the Street of Happiness where the women of the cantinas were.

There she went into cantina after cantina looking for the women Mexicans call "mariposillas." First she showed them the Virgin's statue. This always impressed the women. "Ay how tenderly she looks at us," they cried when they saw the statue. "Madre mia de Guadalupe it even seems like she is smiling."

Doña Chole always looked forward to Saturday. This was

because the cantina women never failed to surprise her with their generosity. Some wept when they gave her all the money they had.

"Take it, little mother," they said. "You're a saintly woman, much too good to even speak with such as we."

Not even the pomaded panders called "Tarzans" who lived on these womens' earnings, objected when they gave the Santera alms. This was because most of the Tarzans had already given Doña Chole alms themselves when she went to the bad death hotels on Mondays.

Saturday night was Doña Chole's best night of the week. On that night she treated herself to a punch called "La Polla" made of milk, eggs, Jerez wine, cinnamon, and sugar. After drinking it, she massaged the varicose veins clotting her rake-handle thin legs with aguardiente. Then she sat in a rocking chair listening to a radio a housewife had given her on one of her Thursday visits to a home near the Parral river.

She purred with contentment, luxuriating in her night of rest, while she listened to Professor Justino Martinez inveigh against the agrarian reform program outlined by Francisco Madero and put into effect by Venustiano Carranza.

She nodded her head in agreement with everything Professor Martinez said.

"Ay, Mexicans no longer fear God," she murmured. "And the peons have become disrespectful."

It was so warm and comfortable in her neatly furnished home that she longed for security so she could sit inside forever. But she realized that she didn't have it and probably never would. This disquieting thought made Doña Chole shake her head mournfully.

So on Sunday she always started all over again.

HOBO SKETCHES

One night in San Antonio, I didn't have any place to stay. The temperature was already below freezing, and the mercury was dropping. It was too late to go to the Salvation Army so I walked around downtown awhile with my cap turned down in ear muffs wishing I had banner money.

The Gunter Hotel had a men's lounge in the basement with an outside entrance. I went to the basement and lay down on a thick rug next to a steam radiator.

I had railroad car lining and cardboard in my chuck sack and I made up an easy-rider mattress. Pretty soon I dozed off with my cap over my eyes.

A middle-aged Mexican porter woke me up long before daybreak.

"You can't sidetrack here," he shouted, shaking me until my cap fell off. "The police will make a nixtamal soup out of you."

But when he saw my face, he stopped shaking me. "Ay, amiguito, you look Indian as Juan Diego—a thousand pardons," he said. "By my mother's ashes, I swear I didn't know we were roosters with the same feathers."

I braced myself on my elbows while my countryman apologized for waking me up. Then he asked me if I was hungry.

"Ay, muchachito, your pants are so ragged your trasero shows in four different places," he said before I could answer. "You need a good menudo between chest and back."

He put a dollar in my hand. I tried half-heartedly to refuse it. But he insisted that I keep it.

"Sufferings with bread are always less, paisa," he said.

After that he took me to the Laredo Cafe to eat pozole and drink vanilla atole.

*   *   *

In the Southern Pacific yards at Lordsburg, I got on a fast run going west with a grizzled rover nicknamed Old Folks.

The train was a highball and had the right of way. When the four-time whistle blew, we were in a gondola loaded with heavy mainline rails.

It was a blistering July day, and the tracks gleamed in the sun like huge watch chains. The gondola bounced over the rough roadbed with a staccato roll burning grease off the ties. Scorching air, bugs, and cinders lashed our faces.

We didn't talk much at first on account of the noise. But just east of Benson, the train went into the hole to let a crack passenger crash by. While the train was holed up, we began talking about something to eat.

"They got a good mission in Pedro," Old Folks told me. "Them tambourine mamas give you all the eggs you can eat."

When I told him my mother lived in El Paso, he nodded approvingly. "They got a good mission there, too," he said. "They give me scrambled eggs and one of them sweet twist rolls for breakfast—only one cup of coffee though."

Then we talked about places we'd been and I mentioned Chicago.

"They give you any meat in them Chicago missions?" Old Folks asked.

When I told him that a storefront mission on West Madison near Desplaines sometimes did, he began talking about going there. He thought that he'd do as well there as anyplace else, maybe better.

"But it don't really matter because ace-duece is the only

number on my dice," he sighed. "A night in the mission, a night in the jail—that's my life."

*   *   *

The boil-out jungle at Indio was strewn with blackened cans and empty bottles of bay rum, wine, and rubbing alcohol. A gray-haired Negro was the only wanderer there when I got in from Yuma on a slow creeper.

When I trudged into the clearing, he was dipping snuff and looking for some place to spit.

"I been dippin' this snuff ever since Hogjaw Mama told me it would stop me from worryin' bout my varicose veins," he explained. "It got a salty taste'n it be's sharp as pepper'n it don't never skeek out the corner of a person's mouth neither."

I sprawled out on a broken icing board and we talked awhile. The old Negro told me hobos called him Drag One because he limped. He said he was going to freight back to Texas so he could get away from West Coast Shorty.

I didn't know who West Coast Shorty was, and I envisioned a glowering bruiser with shoulders big as church doors. But Drag One told me this wasn't so. West Coast Shorty, he said, was just a field hand's nickname for a short-handled hoe.

"Those short-handled hoes will make a man wish he was a rich woman's bulldog," he told me. "I weeded cotton for six weeks in El Centro, and now I'm going back to Lubbock where the wind's strong enough to blow away the mortgage on the widow's old cow, and all the hoes are long-handled."

*   *   *

Across the S.P tracks in Eloy, I went up to a ragtown shanty made out of packing boxes, wallpaper, and sheet iron with bricks laid on the roof to hold it down.

A young Mexican woman answered my knock. I asked her if she had some work I could do. She had a round pretty face and her black hair was done simply and parted in the center. Her eyebrows were straight and black and her white dress made her eyes look darker.

My admiration made her smile mockingly. "It's true I'm oppressed by bad thoughts," she said. "But I have the sainted satisfaction of knowing there are worse than I."

I started to walk away, but she called me back and asked me what my name was. When I told her, she sighed like the saints. "Name of bad luck, all the Amados I know are desgraciados," she murmured. "It seems they're destined to be."

Then she brought me a dish of nopalitos compuestos with a sauce made of chili pasilla. I sat against the rickety shanty and ate wolfishly. While I ate, she rolled a cigarette deftly with her thumb and forefinger and stood against the doorjamb watching me.

Two rigid creases between her eyes gave her a reflective look. Her searching glance made me painfully aware of my ragged pants and the clothesline belt that held them up.

The night before I had tied cords around my pants cuffs to keep the wind out and I had forgotten to undo them. I swung my legs around hoping she wouldn't notice the cords. Then, too, I was ashamed of my hunger at first. But the food was so good, I soon forgot she was watching.

When I finished eating, I thanked her and again asked if I could do some work.

This time she smiled and said: "Not now, paisano. But the next time I want a bank robbed I'll get you to do it."

*   *   *

I picked peaches at Modesto, but I quit after only three weeks. The peach fuzz made my forearms itch and burn and a rash broke out when I scratched them. The weigh hand wished me good luck when I got my time.

"You'll get a better rattle with the dice if you go to L.A.," he told me. "Hope you have better luck on the next roll."

I bought a pound of green chilis and caught a fruit drag for L.A. I carried the chilis in my jumper so I could eat them with beans at Skid Row missions.

At Sister Sylvia's mission, I was eating my chilis with beans when an American man sitting across from me at the board table said: "I don't see how that Mexican can eat them hot peppers without never makin' him a frown." I never knew why I wrote down what he said on a matchbook.

*   *   *

One night in Los Angeles, a kindly Mexican parking lot attendant let me sleep in one of the cars there.

"Ay, Señora Santa, when I was your age, I, too, had nowhere to sleep," he told me."But a taxi driver in Irapuato, Guanajuato kept the trunk of his cab half open so I wouldn't smother, and let me sleep there while he drove all night."

I asked him if he slept well in the taxicab trunk.

"Chavalo, I got my sainted rest when he drove down the Avenida Madero which is paved," was his answer. "But when he drove over the Colonia Rosario's chugholes—ay Madre."

*   *   *

Another night, I jungled under a viaduct off Sixth Street in Los Angeles with a bearded rover who carried a mop handle cane.

We built a chunk fire and began talking about how hard it was to keep clean.

"Bath's to a man what dust is to a chicken," the bearded rover averred. We didn't have any Durham, and after awhile my friend began smoking heavy wrapping paper. When I asked him if he got satisfaction out of smoking paper, he shook his head.

"No, son," he replied wearily. "It's just a heat proposition."

*   *   *

One morning in Fresno, I stood on Tulare Street waiting for a labor contractor nicknamed Wild Grass Woodie to drive a crew of us out to chop cotton. A young Negro called Raggedy Mouth on account of his broken teeth waited with me. A bullhorn was recruiting a crew to tie grape vines and we listened.

"You got found out there, mister?" a hoe hand asked timidly.

"No, you got to find it yourself," the bullhorn snapped petulantly.

"You got any cabins, mister?" the hoe hand persisted.

"No, but we'll sleep you in two old school buses," the bullhorn allowed.

"Mister, you got a little somethin' we can cover up with in them buses?" the hoe hand asked.

"No, it ain't cold," the bullhorn answered.

The bullhorn turned away from the hoe hand and began touting the vineyard owner.

"He's a good Christian—he used to give sheets and he won't let no Sweet Lucys tie grapevines for him," he bawled.

One of the blanket stiffs wanted to know what would happen if a Sweet Lucy went to work there.

"You drink that wine in his fields, you'll have to walk back to town," the bullhorn shouted.

"How far you got to walk if you drink Sweet Lucy, Boss Mister?" Raggedy Mouth asked.

"About twenty miles, boy," the bullhorn replied.

"That cat may be a good Christian," Raggedy Mouth said. "But it's Mississippi Gospel he's preachin'."

The hoe hand started laughing and the bullhorn never did get a crew.

SOMETHING ABOUT TWO HOBOES

When the TP freight train stopped to change crews at Big Spring, the tall, gray-haired hobo got on. I could hear him walking in the cinders outside and I thought at first it was the yard bull coming to kick us off. The two hoboes in the other end of the empty boxcar doused their cigarettes when they heard the door hasp rattling, and I heard them whispering together.

As soon as the door opened I knew it wasn't the yard bull because the moon was bright and it was very light outside, and I could see the man pretty plain. He had long hair, almost like a woman's, and his gaunt face looked blue and frostbitten. He climbed into the boxcar and closed the metal door part way, and I pulled my coat lapels up around my face so the heat from my breath would go down inside my coat and help keep me warm.

The train had started by now and it was picking up speed quick because the ground was level and most all the cars were empty. I could hear the engine puffing real hard, away up front, and the wheels clicking faster and faster over the rail joints sounded like a song, with the rumbling and creaking of the boxcar as a kind of background. It was nice to hear and words like "East" and "West" kept sounding in time to the wheels.

I stood up to look out at the prairie then, and I could see the ground slipping by in a long streak and every little while a telephone pole would flash by. The moon was close up in the sky and it was white and cold and lopsided, and it looked like I could touch it with a long stick.

Across from the boxcar door, the gray-haired man sat all doubled up, smoking a finger-rolled cigarette. After a while he looked up at me, touched his lips with two stiff fingers, and blew imaginary smoke. I nodded and he extended his tobacco sack. When I thanked him, he smiled wanly and asked how I liked running up and down the railroad tracks.

"Don't let your hair grow gray over it, son. It ain't a bad life," he said before I could answer. "After the first couple of years you get numb. You're used to taking a sapping by then, and it don't bother you no more."

The track bed was smooth and the boxcar swayed rhythmically over gnawing trucks and wheels. The gray-haired man bundled up with packing paper and then eased back, planting his palms down on the flooring. After that he told me he had arthritis so bad he couldn't stand up to strongback field work any more.

"When I set down like we're doing now, I have to stand up and wait until the blood starts circulating so it gets down in my legs," he said. "I can't walk until I do that."

The train's speed suddenly slackened and it moved slowly up a grade, its trucks and beams grinding and swishing sluggishly. It seemed to be plowing through a high embankment. The embankment disappeared as if it had been hacked away with an ax, and now the train was paralleling a highway that raced smooth and sharp like a knife blade. The roadbed was rougher, and the train lurched on the tracks. But we talked above the hollow roar of the shaking boxcar, and the gray-haired man said he'd been spot-jobbing through Louisiana.

"I'm too old to sell blood so I been passing handbills when I can," he said. "For a man with bad wheels, that work ain't no stroll though. So mostly I just go to one mission today, and another tomorrow. The mission soup I've eat—with maybe a green bean in it now and then—would fill the Atlantic Ocean. I got to look on the bright side though. I had a good job in Monroe. I worked for Mrs. Pilgrim at her motel and she paid me eight dollars a day. I changed linen and massaged furniture and rugs.

They fire you if you miss a day though, and I had to on account of my legs. She told me she wanted someone who didn't have to lay off every now and then. When I left, her husband said he didn't want to see me go but she was the boss."

The train pounded along the flat grade, lunging past darkened farmhouses and strips of bare field with their patches of plowed land. The wheels began to click faster and faster, and they said "East" and "West" over and over. The din of the moving boxcar heightened, and the wheels were grinding and clashing as if they were going to tear up the flooring.

Just east of Midland, the train went into the hole to let an eastbound hotshot pass and the air brakes under the cars began hissing as if in exhaustion after the long run from Shreveport. The train waited on a siding paralleling the highway, and we could see city lights strung across the horizon. Diagonally across the highway, a half block down, was a lumber yard and a grocery. The side of the grocery had been papered with circus posters, and they were broken and hanging. The lumber yard was the color of goldenrod, and its windows were trimmed in white. In the yard, two men were loading small lumber on a wagon.

The gray-haired man sat with his knees under his chin, and stared across the highway.

"I worked in a lumber yard at Fort Smith a long time ago," he recalled. "I had money in my pocket then."

The prairie wind sliced in through the open door and he turned up his coat collar and blew on his knuckles. But he was chilled through, and he could not stop shivering.

"Now I'm going to El Paso and look for work passing handbills. I like that village," he said. "Last time I was through there, I ate at the Rescue Mission but I didn't sleep there. I saw a truck by a hotel near the train station, and a man and a woman got out of it and went into the hotel. They was drunk, and I knew they wouldn't be up early. So I climbed into that truck and slept sound as a dollar. I slept like a two-year-old in that truck. It was better than staying in the mission basement with all that coughing and stiffs getting up all night long."

He rubbed the sleep out of his eyes with his fists and then smiled, his thin lips barely parting.

"One thing I remember about that mission though. They got a nice little brown dog there," he said. "That little brown dog—a cocker spaniel, I guess—fell in love with me. He jumped up in my lap when he seen me, and I petted him until he fell asleep. When I left, he didn't want me to go."

He pulled his coat collar closer about his neck, and folded his arms tight across his chest.

"I'll tough it out, and see what God says," he mumbled. "But I wish I could find me a job in El Paso and be close to that little dog."

* * *

Another night, I jungled up near the Southern Pacific rip track in Del Rio with a gentle, white-haired rover whose left arm was twisted and paralyzed.

"My arm was paralyzed by high tension wires when I was thirteen," he told me.

The red autumn sun was going down just beyond a rise in the flat farm land. We cooked a monster mulligan in a five-gallon oilcan set on an oven of rocks over the jungle fire, and the white-haired man said he'd lived most of his life with his brother and nieces.

"My brother was a fine man," he said. "He was a widower and me and him made a home for my nieces in Bethlehem, Pennsylvania. I couldn't work in the mills so I kept house for him and helped him raise those two girls. In my spare time, I made up crossword puzzles and anagrams and sold them to weekly newspapers. I made from fifty to ninety dollars a month."

Crow's-feet moved under his eyes when he talked, and a strand of snowy hair fell down across his cheek that still had a sting of color like a winter apple.

"After my brother died and my nieces got married I went on the rail and I been tramping two years now," he said. "It's a dog-eat-dog life on the ramble, ain't it? When you're ragged as we are, people turn away from you. You got to stay sharped up and looking like you was just a fellow about town if you want people to respect you. 'You're just passing through—only not fast enough,' the laws tell me. Me being old and handicapped like this, I'm like a sick dog the flies worry. I can't complain though. Since my brother died, I've seen a lot of the world."

The lonesome dreary moan of a drag whistling the high-ball punctuated the stillness, and the white-haired man said he was going back to Bethlehem and live with a blind friend called the Dutchman.

"I'd rather live with him than go back to L.A. and try to get on the Welfare," he said. "The Welfare's a living death. They sit in those bowl-and-pitcher hotels on the Nickel Street skid row all day."

While the mulligan simmered, he talked about the Dutch-man. "He's spry as you are," he said. "The Dutchman's a lot of fun. He ain't bitter about being blind. He wrote and told me to come live with him and he'd throw his white cane away. He knows every bump in the street and he listens to the Phillies on his transistor radio. He's happy when they win and cross when they lose. Me and him used to go to the Eagle's Club together and people said to him, 'Hello, you old blind bat,' and he joked right with them."

Dusk was smoking out the ebbing glow on the horizon. The white-haired man's palmy hand, swollen by rheumatism, went into his side pocket and got out a crumpled letter written on three-ring notebook paper. When he showed it to me, the smile wrinkles around his eyes deepened.

"You can read what he says for yourself," he invited. "I'm the luckiest man in all the world to have a friend like the Dutchman."

MARÍA TEPACHE

In San Antonio, I got off a Southern Pacific freight train near the tracks that spidered out from the roundhouse turntable. When I quit the train it was almost five o'clock, and the sky was dark with the smoky pall of thunderheads. I was tired and chilled and hungry. I hoped to find something to eat and then get on to Houston.

Nearby was a small white-frame Mexican grocery with a corrugated tin porch held up by a few warped scantlings. The window displayed lettuce heads and coffee in paper sacks, and near the door was a wire bin of oranges. A dog lay on the porch before the door. I went in and asked a buxom, gray-haired woman with a round face and untroubled eyes if she could spare some day-olds.

"Ay, Señora Madre de San Juan, I just fed four hoboes and I can't feed no more," she said.

I started out the door then, but she called me back. She stared at me, her dark eyes becoming very round. "Hijole, paisanito, what spider has stung you—you look sad and burdened like the woodcutter's burro," she said. "Well, I don't blame you. When bread becomes scarce so do smiles."

The gray-haired woman wore a blue dress that was cut straight and came to her knees, and she had on huaraches. She told me her name was María Rodriguez, but she said people all called her María Tepache because she liked Tepache with big pineapple chunks in it so well. We talked of different things—

about where she came from was one. She came from a Durango village populated mostly, she said, by old men, old women, and goats.

"I was born in one of those homes where burros sleep with Christians," she said. "I can read and eat with a spoon, but I'm not one of those women meant to live in homes that would be like cathedrals if they had bells. In our adobe hut village, we lived a primitive life with no more light than the sky gives and no more water than that of the river. But my father never stopped feeding me because he couldn't give me bonbons or clothing me because he couldn't dress me in silks."

She asked me where I was from, her face intent with strong interest. When I told her, she appeared surprised. "¡Válgame San Crispin! I'd never have guessed it," she said.

When I asked why, she smiled and said: "Most Chihuahua people don't talk so fast as we of Durango. But you talk fast, and with the accent of Santa María de todo el mundo."

After that she put on a cambaye apron with a big bow in back, and led me to the back of the store where all the living was done. "This is your humble kitchen—come in," she invited.

The place was like all the homes of poor Mexicans that I'd seen in Texas. There was a broken-legged woodstove, a shuck-tick bed, a straight-back chair, a mirror with the quicksilver gone, and a table covered with oilcloth frayed and dark at the edges. Beyond the stove and to one side was an old cupboard with the doors standing open. The kitchen's bare floor was clean, and the walls were painted wood with only a calendar picture of Nicolás Bravo that hung crookedly from its nail as decoration. On a tiny shelf in a corner was a gilt-framed picture of Maria Guadalupana and a crucified Christ.

The window had burlap curtains, and Doña Maria explained why she put them up long ago. "In a place where there aren't any curtains on the windows you can't expect children to turn out well," she said.

She lit a coal-oil lamp, and set it on the table. Outside it was beginning to rain. Wind blew the rain in through the window and made the lamp burn unevenly and smoke the chimney. The chimney blackened until only a ring around the base gave off light. Doña María closed the window and afterward stood near the lamp and told me she was a widow. Standing there very still with heavy lashes lowered, she spoke of her husband and her voice was husky. The dog that had lain on the porch was curled on the floor by the bed, his head resting on his outspread paws and his eyes watching her.

"In our village my husband was an adobero, and he came here to earn dólarotes in the pecan mills," she said. "I wasn't one of those model Mexican wives who leave their wills in the church, but we were happy together and I never worried that he'd fall in love with another chancluda prettier than me. He couldn't read or write, but I went through the fourth grade at the Justo Sierra School and I taught him about numbers so he could count the stars with our first son. When our centavos married and multiplied, he talked about going back to Mexico. ' ¡Ay Mariquita! If we can go back someday I swear I'll climb Popocatepetl on my hands,' he told me. 'We could go to Puebla on the other side of the volcanoes, and buy land near the magueyes and milpas. We'll buy three cows, and each will give her three litros. Our chilpayates will never dance the Jarabe Moreliano with hunger.'"

Her eyes softened in a reflection of faraway dreaminess. She said her husband made Puebla sound like Bagdad, and talked of singing to her with twenty mariachis.

"Now I live with no more company than my own sins," she said. "I pass my life tending the store, and mending the clothes of my many grandchildren." She broke off and lowered her lids over her eyes, veiling them. Her mouth grew set, a thin, straight line; she passed her hands over her forehead as though awakening from sleep. Her gray hair was in a tangled cloud about her face and she looked older than I'd thought at first seeing her. But when she looked up toward me, she was smiling again and her dark eyes were calm and reflective. "My grandchildren are less brutal than I," she said. "All of them know how to speak the gringo.

I hung my crumpled crush hat on a nail behind the kitchen door and went out in the backyard to split stovewood. The backyard was cluttered with piled-up packing boxes and crates, and the grass was yellow with sand. There was a stumpy cottonwood near the water tap, and a row of sweetpeas clinging to a network of strings tacked on the fence. The cottonwood leaves had turned yellow, but they were still flat with green streaks showing in them. Every once in a while the wind would shake the branches and a flurry of dry leaves and dust funneled up near me.

I split wood, carried out ash buckets, and brought water in a zinc pail. While I worked, Doña María bent over a larded frying pan and told me about her father.

"He was a shepherd and a good man—never ambitious for the centavos," she said. "He was happy and contented with no more ambition than not to lose a lamb and go down to Santiago Papasquiaro two or three times a year to hear the mariachis play in the plaza and listen to the church bells."

When I finished the chores, night was coming and the rain was heavier. There was lightning, vivid flashes that scarred the sky, and I could see San Antonio's lights golden as oil lamps beyond the new Braunfels Bridge. The rain fell through the yellow lamplight streaming from the kitchen window and cars, their lamps wet gems, moved slowly across the high bridge. Their headlights seemed to draw the raindrops, like moths. I looked at them for a moment, rain spattering off my shoulders, then went inside.

Doña María had finished setting the table. She wiped sweat from her forehead with a fold of her apron, and began to fan herself. Then she motioned me to a plate filled with refried beans, rice, and blanquillos.

"Esa es mecha," she said. "It will make you feel like shouting, 'Yo soy Mexicano,' in the middle of a crowded street. Eat— one can think of nothing good when he's hungry."

I ate so fast I grew short of breath. Doña María watched me with her arms wrapped in her apron and crossed over her chest. She looked solemn except for a faint flicker of a smile at the corner of her mouth. The dog sat on his haunches beside her bare legs.

When I finished, she gave me an ixtle shopping bag filled with tamales de dulce, nopalitos, a milk bottle of champurrado, and a tambache of flour tortillas wrapped in a piece of newspaper. I tried half-heartedly to refuse it. But she insisted I take it.

"I have enough for today, perhaps tomorrow, and another day too," she said. "After that, God will say."

When I thanked her, she smiled her mild smile and told me to say the prayer of San Luisito every day.

"May the Indian Virgin who spoke with Juan Diego protect you and cover you with her mantle," she said when I went out the door, "and may you become rich enough to drink chocolate made with milk and eat gorditas fried in Guadalajara butter."

HOBO JUNGLE

In Big Spring, I got off a TP freight train with a veteran fieldhand nicknamed Rails because he had once worked on the railroad. When we quit the train and dropped to the graveled roadbed our numb feet ached from the jar. Snow covered the hip-deep grass of the railroad right-of-way, and the slashing wind off the prairie made my poncho flap and crack like a whiplash. Rails, his face partly hidden by a slouch hat pulled low, walked down the tracks toward the engine, and the crunching of his feet in the roadbed echoed from the dark cars. The gravel was loose and his feet would slip. He brushed a hand before his eyes, as if there were cobwebs.

"It's been so long since I've eat I'd drop dead if you was to shake my hand long enough," he murmured. "I keep thinking about those thirty-cent breakfasts at Hambone's Cafe in Kansas City. Four biscuits, ham gravy, and all the coffee you can drink."

Embers of a jungle fire blinked through frost-browned cottonwoods and brush. We climbed over the coupling pins of a sidetracked boxcar and hurried toward the jungle where mainline hoboes waited to catch out west.

The hobo jungle was a clearing in a stand of low-twisted mesquite trees within a stone's throw of the railroad. It was strewn with blackened cans and broken lugboxes. At its edge was a steep gully at the base of which ran a thin stream.

In the jungle, a small, gray-haired Negro was cooking lima beans in a smoke-blackened lard can propped on stones over a wood fire. His back was bent as if he carried a weight and his cotton trousers were out at the knees, showing other trousers under them. When we stepped into the clearing, he weighed us up with tired unconcern and lifted his hand in salute. His faded eyes, hooded with half-moons of cataracts, looked out of hollow sockets and he held his left arm crooked as if it were in pain.

"Set down and pull up a chair," he invited.

Pale coals studded the mound of dark ashes on the dying fire. The gray-haired man, coughing dryly, scattered the ashes and placed crumpled papers on the coals. The papers blazed and he arranged sticks of wood on the flames. Sparks popped under the dropped wood and we watched the flames lengthen. It was warm except when the wind whistled hard against our backs, and the gray-haired man said he'd rather stand around a jungle fire than stay cooped up in a soup mission.

"I'm rest-broke. I get my best sleep on a rolling boxcar or in a jungle," he said. "They got a pretty good Sally at Aylford and West Third, but I don't like to stand outside Sallies waiting for the praise meetings. People drive by and look at the stiffs and you can tell they're thinking, Look at those lazy bums. They won't work. I got a old piece of carpet and carlining so if I can keep my feet covered and wrap it over my head so's I can breathe I ain't too cold. I'll get some long-distance sleep tonight if the city police don't cat-and-mouse me."

He heaped more wood on the fire and steadied the lard can. When he moved his left arm, lines of pain appeared on his face. He exhaled a sighing breath of tired relief, and picked up his left hand and placed the elbow on his stomach. He talked without gestures, and without opening his lips very far.

"I got neuritis and I can't live up to strongback field work," he said. "But stoop labor's cheaper than ladder work and a stiff'll do better to follow the tree crops. In Wenatchee, they said I was too old to carry the big extension and straight ladders in the apple harvest though. I couldn't get work in the winesaps so I'm looking for a dish job. I've only got a couple of more years of spryness left and I ought to get into a old folks rest home. But in those kind of places you got to do like they say and I can't stay tied up—I get restless. It don't matter though. I could get a 'old' check if I'd set down long enough in one place. But I like to keep moving. A man that's field-tramped all over the country ain't going to be able to set very long. After two or three months he's got to go."

He hitched himself closer to the fire and hunched his shoulders a little, pulling his overcoat collar higher around his throat. Beside him, Rails stared numbly into the shadows that jumped and wavered with the changing flames. The full white moon had risen and was coming over the prairie looking like it rested right upon the sand swells, and it made everything look like silver except in the shadows. The prairie sky seemed to stay blue though, and the stars were white and cold and they didn't wink and twinkle very much. Everything got real quiet and I could hear the fire crackling like little sticks of wood breaking and Rail's slow, thick breathing that was like a deep sigh and the mesquite trees straining against the wind.

The wind blew on the fire and it flared up making everything brighter and I saw a big chesty Negro coming out of the brush and he was walking fast. He was ponderous with bulky shoulders and a strong neck which widened out at the base. He had a round, toothy face and a scar ran down his right cheek like a blister. When he saw us, he smiled sheepishly as though he'd been caught at something he shouldn't have been doing. He had his gaze fixed on Rails and his expression was more analytical than fearful.

"When I saw you-all down the six-foot without no go-way bags I thought you was cinder bulls," he explained. "I'm police-minded because these yards is pretty heavy with tramps and they keep them bulled up pretty good. So I ducked into the brush. I should have known better though. All these Texas-style laws wear cowboy boots and white hats and black suits and shoestring ties around here."

He lit a finger-rolled cigarette, holding the match under his jumper so the wind wouldn't blow it out, and then exhaled with a quick upward jerk of his head. His lips held the curve of a smile, and he gestured at the gray-haired man with his hand. "My buddy's a good jungle quick cook, and he just kept his pot goin'," he said. "Turkey Breast wasn't studying about no yard bulls."

The gray-haired man smiled and replied without turning around. "Big Snead, a yard bull fat as a killing hog, tried to I.D. me last night," he said. "If he meddles me again, I'll bristle up to him and say, 'When was it you last saw your feet, buddy? Yesterday you forgot to tell me.'"

The big man rocked with bursts of laughter, his glaring scar twisting and turning with the contortions of his face.

"Turkey Breast's a trustable buddy. He's well-read and educated and knows spots in the Bible," he said. "On the ramble you meet a guy and travel a division or two with him, and then you never see him again. But me 'n him been hangin' these dirty faces together almost two years now, and we come to all these towns like we was a parade. We been over the roughs and this winter it's seemed like we've had a million miles down a bad road ahead of us. I never could stay at a factory job, but I've always liked field-tramping though. When you pick a tomato or a peach you go to thinking, 'Now some little kid or a family is going to eat this.'"

He brought out a tobacco can and shook two cigarette shorts out of it into the palm of his hand. He extended his palm and Rails took the shorter of the cigarettes and thanked him. Rails's voice was shy, a little shame in it, and the big man, focusing his eyes sharply, stared soberly at him without blinking or shifting his candid gaze.

"Down on your luck, buddy? It makes you feel better to talk with another stiff when you're down on your luck," he said. "The water's rough now, buddy, and a stiff's got to get what he can at this time of year. If he can make his room, board, 'n smokin' he's doin' good. We can't holler calf rope though, buddy. We can't just lay down and die. Hell, we ain't bad off. We ain't sick and we can eat everything we can get a hold of. When choppin' time comes we'll fare fine. We'll come out squared up and with a long stake."

We huddled by the low burning fire talking about farm labor camps and day haulers and blood banks and missions and when TP freight trains went out. Twinkling switch lights dotted the yards like scattered fires, and away to the west, beyond the old salt lake, the hills embossed the sky in a great crawling circle. Somewhere a long way off we heard a train whistle and after a while the straight yellow finger of its headlight poked out of the east. We watched in silence as the engine came nearer and nearer and we heard the heavy coughing of its exhaust die away and knew it was going to stop. When the train left after changing crews, we stood looking after it until the lights of the caboose were faded in the prairie that was still except for the deep coughing of the engine that came to us long after we couldn't see the lights any more. We heard the whistle last.

The gray-haired man fed the fire with twigs so it would burn evenly and not smoke. Wood ash powdered his face, and he said the lima beans were ready.

"The fire wasn't too stout so the limas didn't boil over," he said. "I didn't let them cook in a rolling boil. I just let a bubble come up once in a while. We got one 'n a half pounds of limas in there and I don't want to cook them no more 'cause they're liable to scorch and won't make enough soup for our bread. They're rich as a foot in a bull's mouth now and I'm going to break my bread in them—I won't waste a crumb. We'll get two cookings out of those limas."

The big man rounded his lips as if he were going to whistle and then grinned. He looked at Rails and the grin remained, as if it were fixed about his mouth.

"We got those limas at that Mexican grocery across the Gregg Street viaduct after we changed a tire," he said. "There was this man getting out of a new car by that hognose cafe on First Street, and we asked him if he had a piece of a day's work we could do. He says to me, 'Son, you got a good face on you. You hungry?' I says to him, 'Captain, I could eat a steak with a lamb chop for a pusher. I could eat like I'd borrowed a belly from a horse.' Then he tells us he'll give us a soldier if we'll change his spare tire. 'You look like a good man. You look like a man that would work,' he says to me. 'If you change that tire I'm going to give you a dollar. You can buy yourself some ham trimmings and day-olds or something.' I taken to getting that spare tire out then and I says to him, 'Captain, which one of those wheels do you want us to put it on?' He says to me, 'Son, any one of them will do.' I looks at those tires and I says to him, 'Captain, don't none of those tires need changing.' Then he says to me, 'Son, that is right. I just believe a man ought to earn the money he gets even if he has to just pile rocks from one pile to another.'"

Along the tracks wind-whipped leaves scraped and scurried. The big man touched his scarred face and laughed softly. "That's what I call lucky," he said. "Just changing a tire and earning a soldier. That's what I call lucky. That means we eat."

The gray-haired man turned stiffly and looked at him with a troubled frown. He took his ragged hat off and scratched vigorously at the top of his head.

"Big Snead, me 'n you can't eat those limas and two of us hungry," he said.

The big man picked up a lugbox and ripped off the loosened end slats. In the shadows his body became a huge smudged silhouette and he grinned, rolling his heavy lips back from irregular teeth, and turned his face toward Rails. When he spoke his voice was soft and his gaze, just as direct, was aimed now at an unseen object beyond Rails's shoulder.

"Buddy," he said, "you and your Mexican friend help yourselves—color don't matter."

He opened a loaf of bread and split it into four parts.

BLUE

He was walking down the street with his stringy gray hair hanging down over his eyes, wearing no socks, a toe sticking out of his right shoe, and his heels pushing out of both of them. He had a whittled cane in his left hand and attached to his right hand was a chain with a small dog at the end of it. He stopped and looked at me.

"Where are you going to spend your vacation this winter?" he asked me.

"I don't know," I said. "Any place except here."

"You said it, buddy," he said. "This is the damndest place I have ever seen. I haven't been in town an hour and I have been stopped by the law three times. 'Old Thing, where you going?' they asked me. Yeah, they call you Old Thing around here. It's the damndest town I have ever been in, and it's no wonder hoboes don't get off the trains here. The towners are clannish and they don't cater to freight train stiffs. You're the only stopper I've seen."

"Say," I said to him. "Can't you tell me where we can get a place to eat and sleep around here?"

"No, I can't tell you if there is a mission," he said. "All I can tell you is this is somewhere in Mississippi, and it's a hell of a stop for a tramp. There's more than one way to whip a bear though. Want to go back to the freight yards?"

"Sure," I said.

The overhanging trees of the residential street made a cool

tunnel. At the intersection, the sun was penetrating and warm. The hobo with the whittled cane limped along, his shoes making a scraping rustle on the sidewalk. He had a quiet, gentle face and his rimless glasses were tied around his eyes with two pieces of twine. While we walked, he talked about the blue dog.

"The dog's name is Blue and she's a Australian shepherd," he said. "She's three years old and she's got about eight more years to live. I got her when she was a puppy and she likes riding freight trains. She just puts her head against my leg and goes to sleep. When the train stops, she always wants to jump off but I hold her forepaws and let her down easy so she won't get hurt. I had her vaccinated and she's got her tag. I keep her on a chain though because lots of these cities got leash laws. I turn her loose on the trains, but I tie the chain around my leg when I sleep. She's a good watchdog when anyone comes into the boxcars."

He stopped and pushed a bright, coin-sized piece of metal with his stick. It was tin.

"Me and Blue lost a good friend in Nashville about two weeks ago," he said. "He was a old white tomcat and he died a natural death. He traveled around with us for about six months after he'd been in a accident."

"What kind of an accident?" I said.

"It was a traffic accident," he said. "A truck hit him and broke his leg. That old white tomcat was just about dead when I picked him up in Lake Charles. I got a sandbox for him and taped up his leg and he got well in about a month. He and Blue hit it off fine. He'd lost all his front teeth and he couldn't grind his food though. It don't hardly seem the same without him."

On the sidewalk ahead a group of children were playing, and we turned into the street in order not to interrupt their game. A little girl broke from the group and ran up a path to a house. "Some old bums, Mama. Some old bums," she cried.

We crossed the empty street, and the hobo with the whittled cane said he'd been a knitter in a North Carolina hoisery mill until his eyes went bad.

"I worked there until I was almost forty—that's longer than most do," he said. "Only a young man can see well enough to run a knitting machine. Most of them can count on their eyes giving out on them about the time they get to be thirty years old. Then they have to go back to farming or get on relief."

He asked where I was from. When I told him, he nodded his head and his teeth flashed briefly under his gray moustache.

"That's a good town for stoppers," he said. "If you're busted out and it's cold in El Paso that night clerk at the Army Y will let you sit up in the lobby. Last time I was through there it was snowing, but I didn't go to the Army Y. I went into the McCoy Hotel right next to the Plaza Theater, and eased up to the second floor past the night clerk. There was a lobby there and I laid down on a couch. Somebody had left a cigarette long as a short well-rope there so I had a smoke before I went to sleep."

Just off the railroad property on the north side of town was a small stream, and along its tree-shadowed banks were the blackened cans and flattened ashes of old hobo jungles.

"We can wait for a through-man there, buddy," the hobo with the whittled cane said.

There was a boxlike cafe across the street and on its windows were lettered short order: "Chili, 25¢ . . . Soup, 30¢ . . . Two Eggs any style, 40¢."

"I'm going in there and try to stir up something," he said. "I'll ding-dong some ice cubes. Blue likes icewater."

I looked after the blue dog while he went into the cafe. When the door closed behind him, an unmarked prowl car carrying two plainclothesmen nosed into the curb.

"Come here, Old Thing," one of the plainclothesmen said to me.

He had a long face. It looked like a big capsule. I got out my alien registration card so he'd know I wasn't a wet Mexican.

He looked me up and down and then said: "Old Thing, where you going?"

"To catch a freight train," I said.

"All right," he said. "You catch your train over there. Which way you going?"

"To California," I said.

"Going to enjoy yourself?" he said.

"No," I said. "I'm going to top carrots at Indio."

The plainclothesmen drove off. The hobo with the whittled cane came out of the cafe with ice cubes in a paper cup. He grinned good-naturedly and said there was some wood piled up against the side of a gulch near the jungle. We went for the wood. It was stuck back in the honeysuckle vines and nobody would ever notice it, but he knew where it was. Most of it was charcoal wood that wouldn't show any smoke and would make a hot fire, but there was some pine wood, too, for kindling.

We brought the wood up to the jungle. The fire crackled right up, and we sat down in front of an oak tree that must have been six feet through at the base. The sun was close down on the horizon that was far away, and we watched it sink out of sight while the sky faded through its different soft colors that were like washes. All there was to do was to wait for a train that would stop so we could get on to Louisiana. Two passenger trains came and went while we waited. One went north and the other rumbled across a bridge and on south. Neither of them stopped and we just smoked cigarettes and waited. The blue dog was beside us drinking from the paper cup.

It was twilight then and there was a dark red look to the sky in the west where the sun had gone down. After awhile the black sky in the east began to sweep over and blot out the day's last blue. Pretty soon the North Star came out, and then it was night. It was almost December, but the night air wasn't very chilly. There was a cool breeze though and it lifted the cinnamon vines a little so that they swayed on their gnarled stems.

The hobo with the whittled cane rolled another cigarette and offered me the tobacco and paper, but I shook my head and used one of my own Mexican cigarettes. He smiled and squatted on his heels by the oak tree and watched the blue dog as she drank.

"Me and Blue went to this mission in Jackson the night before last," he said. "The tramp doorman didn't want to let Blue in, but one of the Bible guys made him. That made the tramp doorman mad and he growled at me under his breath, 'If you ain't a Christian I hope this meal makes you sick enough to die,' he told me."

He took a deep drag from his cigarette and looked at the curled toes and grass-filled wrinkles of his scarred shoes. Then he tore flaps from a cardboard box and cut out new soles and wrapped them with paper and put them inside his shoes.

"I'm one of those old whiskers tramps that wears something patched, tied, hooked, or wired," he said. "You don't see many oldtimers like me in the weeds any more."

He got up and stood by the fire with his hands hanging down by his sides, loose as arms stuck on a scarecrow. His face was vacuous with waiting, and he reached up with his right hand and pushed the hair out of his eyes. Then he sighed and smiled at me.

"That was a miss-meal sigh, buddy," he said. "I keep thinking about French fried potatoes. I can eat them by the panful."

I had a dollar. I said I'd get something at a mom-and-pop grocery. But he shook his head.

"Buddy, don't get nothing for me," he said. "I can make it to New Orleans."

He smiled his mild smile at me, and his teeth showed dimly under the gray moustache.

"I'd be uncommonly grateful if you was to get some dog food for Blue though," he said.

TWO SKID ROW SKETCHES

In St. Louis, I stood in the doorway of the Sunshine Mission with a small, pale rover who wore an old broadcloth coat fastened together with safety pins.

The full-house poster was up at the mission, and we could not go inside. Snow was coming down slowly and silently in front of the bright staccato flashes of neon along the Franklin Street skid row. The mercury had dropped to two below zero, and street crews were spreading calcium chloride on the icy thoroughfares. It was quiet. We began to notice how quiet it was.

"It's too bad we come late," the small hobo said. "Sometimes they give you a pot of navy beans in there—a regular potful. The service is short too. That preacher don't hold you too long."

He was polite with a soft voice and a gentle manner. His face was very white and very thin with eyes so deep-set that the shadows around them looked like bruises. When he spoke, his forehead wrinkled as though it hurt him to think and he breathed in jerky, agitated breaths.

"Me'n you got to do something before long," he said. "We got to make a move pretty soon. If we stay in this doorway we'll freeze."

He had begun to feel the cold more; his face was twitching. He hunched his shoulders and shivered. "Pancho, there's a grate in that alley back of the Salvation Army Harbor Light Center and warm air blows up through it from the Sally's basement," he said. "We can go there and sit on that grate when the praise meeting ends at the Sally. It's like sitting on a stove."

He stopped speaking, his voice fading into a void as though he had suddenly grown tired. He stood hunched over, breathing heavily, and his right hand opened and closed repeatedly, as though it were clutching something tightly, then quickly letting it go. He tried to say something and his mouth opened but no sounds came out and he stood very still for a moment. His breath came lagging. It faltered. Then it came steadily again.

When he caught his breath, he spoke again, low, as if he had been running hard. He said that he was not sick, he had no pain, but all of a sudden he felt weak, tired, and sleepy from the cold of the night and the noise and speed of the Missouri Pacific freight which he had ridden from Kansas City. His voice was toneless, carrying nothing but a faint breathlessness. He said he couldn't stop thinking about how good he'd had it in Bakersfield the winter before.

"Pancho, I made it good there," he said. "I couldn't catch a day haul in the carrots so I got lawed for loitering and did a bit on the Kern County Road Camp. But I had a good go. We eat Southern home-cooked food there. Every morning there was big gallon cans of hot syrup and hot cakes and fried potatoes on the table, and there was lots of toast and pots of coffee and boxes of dry cereal. For dinner and supper there was plenty of turnip greens and I eat a lot of roasting ears too because some of the other prisoners had bad teeth and didn't want them. Besides that my fall buddy's aunt sent him boxes of Baby Ruth candy and me'n him eat five or six candy bars a day. We eat like better-living people and just did a little clean-up work. I wish I was back in that three-quarter bed I had at the road camp tonight."

The wind swept into the doorway from the Mississippi River. The mission windows rattled faintly. He shivered and his gaunt face grew reminiscent.

"When I think about it, I can feel the steam heat coming up through the sideboards," he said.

* * *

In Los Angeles, a legless transient with a silver birthmark streak in his hair asked me to wheel him out to the SP yards so

he could get on a northbound freight train. "Pancho, I'm wore-
out and I got to get some rest," he said. "I haven't laid down in
a week, and I'm just a jump ahead of a fit. I want to ball the jack
out of here. Last night I tried to stretch out in that open-air
parking lot next to the big bus station at Sixth and Los Angeles
Streets. But the ants was so bad I had to get up from there. Before that I set up six nights in the bus station. Those security
officers in the admirals' uniforms let me set there, and I nodded
and dozed a little in my wheelchair. They didn't ask me to show
a bus ticket."

He was thin and the blue under his eyes was deep. His
skin was taut, like parchment, over bouldery cheekbones and he
had on a black coat sweater. He said he'd had a sandwich two
days before and that was the last time he'd eaten.

"It was a big sandwich," he said. "You know that place on
Central Avenue where they sell French fried hot dogs and pig
hots. I was hungry and broke so I went into that place just to
look at those foot-long hot dogs. A colored waitress come up to
take my order. I said: 'Miss, what would you do if I told you I
couldn't pay for one of those foot-long hot dogs?' She said: 'You
broke, mister? Well, you just take one of them.' 'Can I do some
work for it? That front window looks dusty,' I said. She said; 'No
mister, you better go because if the boss was to come and see
you with that hot dog he'd wonder why there wasn't nothing in
the cash register.'"

We moved up the Fifth Street skid row toward Main Street.
It was still dark with only a little light beginning to show in the
sky. I pulled my coat collar up around my ears, but it did no
good. The chill came from my soggy feet and the wind that
howled around the corner.

"I tried panhandling, but I couldn't score enough for a
bed," the legless man said. "When I panhandle, I don't have to
tell them a fairy tale and use my imagination. This is the best
story for panhandling I got—me without legs and in a wheelchair.
I'm not even a good semipanhandler though. Last night I tried
to ding-dong them on Broadway after the shows let out. But a
plainclothesman big enough to go bear hunting with a switch run
me back to the skid row. He told me not to worry the people."

He straightened up, shivering, and fumbled with shaking fingers for his Durham sack. He rolled a cigarette with a snapping motion of his thumb and forefinger, licked it, and held it straight up while he caught the round pasteboard tab on the tobacco sack's yellow drawstring between his lips. When he had the cigarette burning, he said he'd ridden more freight trains since he'd lost both of his legs than he ever had before. "I ride with the train crews now," he said. "The trainmen have helped and re-helped me. I go to the dispatcher and tell him I got to travel. The dispatcher generally introduces me to the crew, and they most always let me ride in the caboose. The crew has a good atti-tude toward me so I eat good and they bring me what I need. I get some relief on the trains. That's my way of life now." The slate sidewalk was still wet and it looked silvery in the wan morning light. The legless man turned his head, the smoke from the cigarette creeping through his shut lips in a flat, even line. He spoke wearily as though he were expelling a breath he had been holding.

"It's thin gravy for me in the cities," he said. "You get treated bad when you're broke. Sometimes I get so hungry I can't even talk. I don't like to go to the stopper joints here in L.A. though. It's a big dropoff town, but there's no good stops for tramps here. They're not like that no-knock mission in Port-land where they give stiffs a half gallon of cider and all the apples they want."

He lowered his head and began to rock it, just perceptibly, from side to side. The tendons of his sinewy neck played into two bony knots behind each ear and his black hair grew long and curling.

"I'm not a fellow that likes to have somebody plan every hour of my life for me," he said. "In those stopper joints you got to get up when they say up; go to bed when they say go to bed; eat what they hand you to eat and swallow it when they say swallow. Besides that, they're so crowded you can't cuss the cat without getting hairs in your teeth. I got a better go on the rail-road. I don't have to wait in line for hours for a bowl of soup and stale bread."

Dawn was coming slowly. We could not see the sun, but a distant cloud was beginning to glow. The legless man bundled up in his freight train blanket and stared at the pavement with dark eyes brilliant from lack of sleep. He sat with his narrow shoulders hunched and his hands crossed and thrust up his sleeves. He looked as if he couldn't see anything clearly, as if everything were strange.

"The worst that can happen to anyone is not to be able to eat and sleep," he mumbled.

We left Main Street and moved down the San Fernando Road in the direction of the Glendale yards. It was frosty and the edges of my cap were white. There were puddles all over the road in the low places and they were frozen over. The wind was blowing from the northwest and it was a strong, raw wind. It was almost spring, but it felt like a day in January.

"I get some good long-distance sleep in the caboose," the legless man said. "It's warm as daytime and sometimes I lay down on the leather couch. Other times I wrap myself around the small-bellied cookstove like a cat and sleep ninety miles an hour. It's like being in a warm bed with the covers pulled up tight around my chin. I don't always ride in the caboose though. Sometimes the crew wheels me up to the head-end of the train and puts me in one of the diesel units. I sit in the lean-back chair by the window and just look out until I get sleepy. Then I stretch out on the decking.

"When the head-end brakeman comes in to check the diesel gauges, he usually adjusts the heat for me and there's always plenty of drinking water in that big Distillata jar they keep there. The brakeman just tells me not to touch the diesel instruments. I eat good there too. The crew cooks it in the caboose and brings it to the engineer and the head-end brakeman. It's good food too, not like deepwater soup at the missions. The crew cooks solid meals like restaurants do. I'd rather eat on those trains than have breakfast with the president."

He smiled with his eyes almost shut.

"Last time I eat three different kind of vegetables," he said.

HELPING HANDS

In Bakersfield, I spent my last dime for a cup of hot champurrado at a small Mexican café near the Rescue Mission. A middle-aged Mexican waitress served me. She was short and plump, and her hair was like black silk bound around her head. She wore Patzcuaro earrings adorned with silver fish, and she smiled when I looked at them.

"I'm from Pátzcuaro," she said proudly. "I'm more Pátzcuarense than the lake."

My ragged clothes embarrassed me so much I did not want to talk. But my silence made her smile all the more.

"I can see you're not one of those young men whose glances turn women into meek lambs," she said. "But don't be afraid of me, joven. I don't have horns. Neither animals nor men have anything to fear from me."

She asked what I was doing in Bakersfield. I told her I had come to pick peas. But I explained I had come too early. The peas had not filled out yet, and were still flat. The harvest would not begin for another week.

She nodded sympathetically. "To go without work is to die of hunger," she said. "I'll burn a candle to the Virgen de los Dolores for you. She's a pearl and she'll help you. She's not one of those ugly santas that frighten children."

When I finished my champurrado, she asked if I wanted anything more.

"No, señora, that's all," I said.

I got up to go then, but she said, "Wait, joven," and

brought me chiles rellenos, Campechanas, and more champurrado.

When I thanked her, she smiled and said, "That's all right, joven, I know how it is to be broke."

*   *   *

Another night in Bakersfield, I went into the bus station on Twentieth Street to get out of the rain.

I leaned back on a bench and stretched my feet in guarded relaxation. After a while I dozed off. But a burly security officer shook me awake. He had a lumpy, double-chinned face with broken and tobacco-stained teeth. His shirt was tight and I could see the heavy back muscles bunched under his shoulder blades.

"Son, what bus you waiting for?" he asked, and his stolid face cracked slightly with a difficult smile.

"None, sir," I said. "I just came in to get out of the rain."

"Son, you're too ragged to be sitting around here," he said. "All these people are looking at you."

He gave me fifty cents and told me to get back to the Southern Pacific yards.

*   *   *

At another hobo jungle near the old ball park in East Chattanooga, a little Negro girl with tightly braided pigtails brought me a big bag of food.

"Mama told me to bring you this," she said. "She thought you might be hungry."

It was cold and her breath smoked in the chilly air. I thanked her and began eating the food. She smiled and then hurried across a dust road to a board cabin with two windows and one door. A stout woman wearing a housecoat and flat bedroom slippers was standing by one of the two-by-four scantlings which supported the porch roof of the cabin. I guessed she was the little girl's mother. But I was too ashamed to go over and thank her on account of my ragged clothes.

*   *   *

In Santa Monica, I was sitting on a stone bench in an ocean-front park filled with elderly people when a lanky policeman with a hard, seamed face got off a three-wheeler and came up to me. He asked for identification, and I showed him my alien registration card.

"Muro, I've had a complaint about you," he said after looking at the card. "Some of these people say you're not presentable enough to be around here. These are pretty high-class people, and you've got a freight train blanket and a week's growth of beard. Have you looked at yourself in the mirror lately?"

When I told the policeman I was a fieldhand and hadn't come there to panhandle, he shrugged.

"My advice is to stay out of these nice places and get on back to LA's Nickel Street skid row," he said. "If you don't, I'll have to latch you up."

He got back on his three-wheeler and waited for me to move on. I slung my freight train blanket over my shoulder and started to walk away. But a stocky, thick-shouldered man whose muscled bulkiness clashed with his boyish face stopped.

"Having it tough, eh, buddy?" he asked.

The stocky man wanted to know why the policeman had questioned me. When I told him, he said, "These are a particular bunch of old people. No doubt you're hungry—take this."

He handed me a dollar and walked away. Along about that time the policeman honked his horn, and I didn't have a chance to thank him.

*   *   *

In Fresno, I made two dollars scrapping ground cotton for Cadillac Jack, a farm-labor contractor. The next day I went out for another day hauler nicknamed Uncle Bill and made a dollar topping carrots before rain drove us out of the fields. But the following morning I couldn't catch a day haul.

That night, when the Tulare Street skid row's hazy demiworld came to life, I stepped into a flophouse doorway to get out of the clammy tule fog. I hadn't been there long when a car carrying three boys nosed into the curb and one of them bawled, "Hey, tramp, want to make twenty cents? Buy us some beer."

The boys jeered at my ragged coat, which would have scared crows in any cornfield, and drove off. I started toward the Southern Pacific yards then, hoping to hole up in a weather-breaker shed until time for the Blood Bank to open. But a cheery old hobo, who had a bread wrapper knotted around his head like a bandana, stopped me. He was small and spindly with bony ridges above his gray eyes and diamond-shaped wrinkles on the back of his weathered neck. His scarred shoes were laced with pieces of string and he wore horn-rimmed glasses which had only one earhook left, so that he had to hold them up to his eyes with one hand. He smiled and asked if I was a Mexican.

When I nodded, he said, "Name's E. J. Watters—two *t's* in Watters. I got hold of a few nickels. You hungry?"

The kindly old rover offered to buy me a meal. He explained why.

"I'm a hardtack panhandler and Mexicans have always helped me," he said. "So after I score at a Mexican home I'm every Mexican's brother and sister."

He led me to the Mexicali Café near China Alley. On the way, he told me he got a small old-age pension, but couldn't stop running around the country.

"I got a check coming now, but Nellie—that's my sister—don't know where to send it," he said. "I have to live wild. I can't stay in one place very long. Age has slipped up on me, but I don't want to sit in a park with other old pensioners all day. I like to hustle—the struggle keeps me alert. I been swinging on the trains all my life, and I still got it in me to go for a ride. It's the humor in your blood. A freight train stiff's got to be gone. His brain's overtaxed."

We went into the Mexicali Café. The café was high and narrow, its tiled floor sprinkled with sawdust, its ceiling of pressed metal painted blue. Down one side were several white-topped tables, down the other the counter. A young Mexican waitress smiled at us when we straddled mushroom stools at the counter. She had dark eyes and her shoulder-length hair, loose and luxuriant, was waved in a high cluster of curls set off by butterfly earrings. She took our orders and her lips were red against the whiteness of her teeth when she smiled. The old rover bought me a torta de huevo, refried beans, corn tortillas, and coffee with piloncillo. While I ate with unabashed gluttony, he talked about panhandling.

"This old tramp knows how to get by," he said. "I stood outside the bus station yesterday so I could get them coming and going, and I didn't miss many. I said 'beg pardon' so often I woke up last night saying it. I dreamed I was bracing somebody. I put it to them straight. I don't whine or appeal in a pitiful way when I panhandle. I go up to them and say, 'By God, I bet I'll be eighty afore you will,' so they smile and get that charitable feeling. If you go up to them with a smile and look them in the eye you'll make it. You'll take abuse, but you'll come out. One of them said to me, 'I don't give money to bums.' I said to him, ' "That's all right and God bless you, sir. The world don't owe me a living, and I wish you well.' I walked away then, but he whistled me back and said, 'Nobody ever approached me like that. God damn your time, Dad, you're all right.' He give me five dollars."

He saucered his coffee and watched a bull cook splash another egg into a skillet already popping and sputtering with them.

"It's pretty hard for a confirmed panhandler to break away from the game," he said. "I've got rid of my pride and it's second-nature to me now. Sometimes I think about laying down to die, but it's my way to make a living. It's determination to survive or just a way of life—I don't know which but I'm good at it. Everyone's got to be good at something, even dreaming. It's hard to analyze. It's pretty hard to like something that people look down on. I must like it or I wouldn't do it though. It grows on you."

The jukebox was playing "Siete Mares." The music ended and the machine made a clicking sound and was still. The Mexican waitress moved around the cash register and presently the coin slot jingled and then the machine was playing again: "Siete Mares." The old rover straightened his back, flexed his neck, and then said he was going to Troop, Texas, when the weather warmed up.

"There's too much pushing and pulling in California," he said. "I want to breathe, and Troop is a good payoff town for me. If a panhandler can't make it there, he can't make it nowhere. There's a lot of cheese-and-cracker folks in that village, and it's the only place I know where they'll give a stiff a piece-off without him asking them for it. I stood in the rain there looking forlorn and six of them handed me anywhere from thirty-five to seventy-five cents. Then a law come along and showed me his badge and told me to stop worrying the people. He said, 'Old Man, let them alone.' I looked at his badge and said to him, 'Officer, that don't cut any ice—I got to eat same as you do and smoke.' He give me fifty cents and then said, 'Don't let me see you bum them no more.' I said, 'I can't promise that because I'll be after them when you're gone. You'll have to turn your head.' He laughed then and told me to go ahead with my ding-donging. After that I went into a café and **asked a waitress with silver-dyed hair how much coffee was.** She said, 'Ten cents.' I said, 'Well, I guess I can afford that.' She said, 'You poor old man—is that all you've got?' and she fed me."

When I finished eating, he paid the check and left a tip for the Mexican waitress.

"Now I'm going out and do some more ding-donging," he said. "I'm going to hit them hard. I ain't going to be lenient on them. This old tramp won't take *No* for an answer tonight."

We shook hands and I thanked him. But he waved my thanks aside.

"Names E.J. Watters—two *t's* in Watters," he said. "Just holler next time you see me."

MORE HOBO SKETCHES

In Big Spring, I chopped stovewood for a young Mexican house-wife who lived in a tumbledown shanty near the east yards. When I told her I came from Parral, Chihuahua, she smiled and said she, too, was from a Tarahumara Sierra village. She hadn't, she said, been in Texas long. Her husband had come to Big Spring only a few months before to work on a TP gandy gang. While I hacked slivers out of fruit boxes for the fire, she sat on the flat rock doorstep and told me about him.

"Water is my Hilario's only drink," she said proudly. "He's not one of those men who open their mouths better for drinking than praying. He'd rather talk with me than go to cantinas. Never have I mourned our marriage." But, she said, they sometimes quarreled about the way she wore her hair. "He wants me to have my hair bobbed so I'll look muy catrina like the gabachas," she told me.

When I asked why she didn't have her hair bobbed, she blushed and said: "Ay chavalo, our village priest Father Romero once told me the noblest, healthiest, and least bad-intentioned caress a man can give a woman is to stroke her hair and a woman with a boyish bob will never know this."

* * *

In Los Angeles, I made four dollars a day passing bills. But after a month the soles of my scarred shoes worked loose and flopped up and down when I mailmanned. I tied them to the toes of my shoes with string, but the string wore through and a day or two later I developed bill-passer's blisters. The blisters were so bad I couldn't doorknob any more. When my rent fell due at Scotty's Flophouse on Fifth Street, I couldn't pay it.

Scotty's Flophouse was a dark rickety warren cut up by wooden partitions into many rooms and dormitories. I didn't want to give up my cot and two heavy horse blankets there. The flophouse day clerk, bald and paunchy with a blotchy, razor-burned face, had always been friendly with me. But when I asked him to let me sleep there until my blisters healed, he laughed.

"Muro, you won't read a better joke than that in a book," was his answer.

When I insisted my credit was good, he stared meaningfully at my thready jumper and drainpipe pants that belled at the ankles. "It'll be good when you're eighty years old and come back here with your mother," he said.

*   *   *

That night I jungled up under the Broadway Bridge with a veteran rover nicknamed C and O Dad because he had worked on Chesapeake and Ohio gandy gangs.

C and O Dad, tall, gaunt, and white-haired, was a cheery man of bizarre contrasts. Too independent to stay in missions, he wandered city streets panhandling with shrill eloquence. When he wasn't panhandling, he hustled toy flags attached to placards with "Lest We Forget" in big letters and "Sold by a Disabled Veteran" in smaller letters.

After we built a fire with the wheel packing and broken lug boxes, he showed me a bag of his flags. He said he bought them at novelty shops and sold them outside supermarkets. "The housewives most always rattle their coins," he averred. "You'll go a long way before you find a prettier little grift than flag hustling."

We smoked and talked while he darned his socks by the

firelight. "Son, we're doves without nests—we're twelve ways from the jack," he said. "We move through big cities like ants in forests and attract about as much attention."

We talked while the fire burned lower and lower until there was nothing left but a few embers without heat. After that we bundled up in carlining. The hollow thunder of cut cars rolling down the blind track lulled C and O Dad to sleep. But hunger kept me awake. Once I got up to look at the wild berry vines that covered the sides of the railroad right-of-way ditches. But there were no berries on the vines. C and O Dad woke up and advised me to forget about them. "We'll get us a bellyful at Hogjaw Mama's Cafe in the morning," he promised. "She'll put the pancakes and sausages to us. That big Nigra woman feeds more long-distance stiffs than Sister Sylvia's Mission does. She always says 'C and O Daddy, sit down and eat enough for tomorrow' and I always tell her 'That'll be hard, Hogjaw Mama, 'cause I ain't eat enough for yesterday yet.'"

When I thanked C and O Dad for the meal in advance, the smile creases on his bristly face deepened.

"Son, I'd do anything in the world to help one of you strange-tongue stiffs," he asserted. "But I'm lyin', I'm dyin', if I'd ever harm a Mexican that's on the blink."

All night long I thought about hotcakes and coffee. The prospects of a good breakfast appeared almost too good to be true. But when we got to Hogjaw Mama's Central Avenue Cafe at daybreak, everything turned out the way C and O Dad had predicted. The globular colored woman grinned when C and O Dad shambled into her cafe. She put two steaming cups of coffee on the counter, and bawled an order to the bull cook.

"C and O Daddy, you and your Mexican friend jest set yourselves down here in Millionaire's Row and eat enough for tomorrow," she invited.

And C and O Dad said: "That'll be hard, Hogjaw Mama, 'cause we ain't eat enough for yesterday yet."

*   *   *

Along about that time a cold wave swept in and the Bread of Life Mission let homeless men sit up in the chapel all night. I sat up with about 300 other vagrants who had no place else to go. In the chapel, a one-armed mission stiff with a long, nickeled flashlight kept derelicts from sprawling out on the benches. Signs reading "Sit Up" were posted on the high windowless walls, and the one-armed spotter enforced them.

When weary rovers sagged, he beamed his flashlight in their faces and glared at them fiercely as though trying to remember their features before he destroyed them. On account of him nobody slept much. But the chapel was warm and it was cold outside. So vagrants, who needed good food and warm beds to take the paleness from their skins and fill up the hollows of their cheeks, sat up and talked most of the night.

One night I sat next to a small, pale man who looked sick. His face was dry and gray like school tablet paper, and his beard looked dark against his bloodless skin. We didn't talk much until he drew a loaf of bread on the margin of a religious tract and then printed "Easy to Draw but Hard to Get" underneath it. When I laughed about the drawing, he leaned closer and confided that he had lost his road buddy. The buddy had braced a plainclothesman on Spring Street and was in the Lincoln Heights Jail for panhandling. The pale man told me he missed him. They'd been road buddies, he said, ever since they had been in Los Angeles County Hospital together. He said they'd had it good there.

"In our ward they give us meals like better-living people eat," he averred. "Me'n him eat a dozen eggs for breakfast sometimes—blanket stiffs who'd been operated on didn't want them."

The pale man said he worked when he could at hard dollar jobs that required stooping, digging, cutting, pulling, climbing, and lifting in the rain, dust, heat, and cold. "But I never have made a real living at farm work or gandying—it's been dog after rabbit," he said, "I just keep a jump ahead of starvation."

He said he'd like to find a job in one of the big downtown office buildings where men go to work dressed like it's Sunday. "If I worked in one of them places I'd go to the show every night and buy at least two detective story magazines every week," he said. "But a stiff won't find them kind of jobs in the Want Ads."

We talked all night and he spoke of his boyhood in Cleveland's Parmadale Orphanage. He said he and his brother had been happy there. "I think about how happy we was every time I sit up in a mission or carry the banner," he said. "The Sisters of Charity seen that we got three meals a day all during the depression—we was better off than most. That was more than I had when my father was alive, and it's more than I've ever had since."

*   *   *

One night I got off a slow drag in Yuma with a friendly countryman nicknamed Medianoche because he was dark. We were hungry and cold so we beelined for the mission. On the way we talked about gorditas, atole, and chalupas—the hungry Mexican's dream of heaven. After a while my countryman shrugged wearily. "We'll make the burros laugh with this kind of talk, paisa', " he said. "We got to eat whatever the Reliefers lay out—done or raw."

But we never got to the mission because Medianoche found a nickel. He whacked me on the back and held it up so I could see it.

"Ay Chihuahua, cuanto Apache," he exulted. "Now we can nickel up, paisa'—nickeling up's hard to beat when stiffs are hungry."

After that we looked for a Mexican grocery. Near the double deck ice docks we found one. The grocer, short, stocky, and graying, was playing the "Corrido of Juan Reyna" on a windup phonograph. "Muchachos, I like the songs written by paisanos who blew Zapata cow horns," he told us.

That was when Medianoche nickled up. He asked for five cents worth of stew meat. When he said that, the grocer put on his pinch-nose glasses and looked into our lackluster, blood-veined eyes inflamed by cinders and face-cutting winds.

"Muchachos, I, too, once knew the pains of tramping

Mexico's roads looking for work," he said. "I, too, had to move heaven and earth to make a living."

He asked us where we were from, and how long we had gone without eating. When we told him, he turned quickly and picked up a brown paper bag but his movements after that were unhurried. He filled the bag with stew meat, vegetables, green chiles, a soup-bone, and pinole. Then he shoved it across the counter.

"Con Dios, muchachos," he said. "May you earn more and sweat less."

We thanked him and hefted the bag outside thinking about the things blanket stiffs do to beat hunger. Only hungry stiffs ever nickled up at groceries. When Medianoche ordered five cents worth of stew meat, the kindly grocer knew the nickel was all we had. We wanted him to know that because some people won't take a hungry stiff's last nickel. Some people will give a stiff what he asks for and something besides. They have had troubles of their own, and they know how it is to be hungry. The grocer was one of those people.

"May God give him a good place in the sky," Medianoche said, signing the cross. "Now we can stew up at the boil-out jungle by the river—they got good tincans there, and there aren't no ranch dogs, paisano."

I thanked him, envisioning caldillo simmering in one of the gallon cans hoboes call gunboats. But Medianoche waved my thanks aside and said: "It wasn't nothing, paisa'—even a blind pig will stumble across an acorn now and then."

ROAD BUDDY

One night I slept in the Southern Pacific sandhouse at Tucson. When I woke up, it was growing light. Up the tracks a bell clanged and boxcars rattled together. I jumped over an iron switch post and ran for a freight train red-tagged for L.A. The train, a doubleheader, was just pulling out and the sing in the rails told me it was a hot one. It jerked violently and then seemed to stretch in a sudden pickup of speed while I ran hobbled by my back pack. The engine and a dozen cars passed me before I knew it. There weren't any good rides so I had to try for a flat car. Beside that the train was balling and I wasn't sure I could swing it. But a burly hobo with a Barbary pirate's moustache was on the flat car. When he saw me running alongside, he arose stiffly and helped me up the grab irons.

"Hurry up, Pancho, your Pullman won't wait," he shouted while I scrambled up.

Once aboard I could see sparks fly when the brake shoes bit into the wheels. The train rocked like a ship, its trucks and beams grinding, and the wheels began clicking in heightened speed. The burly rover told me it was red hot.

"This one's a fast guy—he's been battin' plenty all the way from Santone," he said. "He's some rambler—stays right on the main."

He stretched out on the warped floorboards with guarded slowness, pillowing his head on his arm. His bridgeless nose was mashed flush with his face, and his shoulders looked a yard wide.

He had on a gray snapbrim hat which had been trimmed with scissors, and his clothes were just rags pinned and tied together. But his heavy face, road-seared and rough as oak bark, was serene with quiet good nature and he weighed me up with a smile.

"You're on the floor, ain't you, Pancho," he said after studying me. "Well I ain't worried about my social standing neither—I forgot to put on my silk tie."

When I told him I was on my way to pick Kern County potatoes, he nodded approvingly and wished me luck.

"I knowed you was a work beast," he averted solemnly. I could tell you wasn't no blindsider."

We talked for a while and he told me he'd been fruit tramping most of his life, following the tree harvests and steeple-jacking in the dates. He said once he'd tried to take a step up the social ladder, but the rung broke.

"I had a good job with Boeing Aircraft in Seattle, but when the cherries got ripe I went off fruit tramping again," he said. "It don't matter though—a hungry eagle's happier than a well-fed rooster." The smile wrinkles around his eyes deepened and his roughly weathered face grew reminiscent. "I used to dress like a headwaiter when I had that Seattle job," he said. "But I can't quit the road—I got it in the marrow of my bones."

The train began to bounce violently and he sat up, lifting himself on his hands until the bumping lessened, and then he lay down again.

"There's something primitive about tramping that I like—I ain't no Skid Row steady," he said. "A road-broke stiff like me has to keep moving. When a stiff keeps moving, he'll always run into something—a flop, a handout, a piece of change. All a stiff's got to do is keep moving." He said he'd never wanted to settle in any particular town. He told me he liked them all. "Each new town makes me forget the others," he said. "They're like girls."

When I thanked him for helping me swing the train, he smiled again and offered me a drink of water from a wine bottle covered with bicycle tape. After that we settled down for a long, bumpy ride. The redball was riding a noisy load and we didn't

talk for some time. Then hunger seized me almost without warning, and with a vicious, shaking grip. It was as if a draining needle
had been plunged into me, and my strength-emptied body
trembled.

I tried to make my legs work, but the sky was spinning. I
lifted my hand and watched it shake. My back ached and my
stomach felt hot. Sweat slid off my face like thin oil.

The burly rover had tied a bandana around his neck so
cinders wouldn't get underneath his shirt. But when he saw how
I was sweating and trembling, he undid the bandana and swabbed
my temples with it.

"Pancho, you got a fever fit to blister your forehead," he
said.

He asked if I'd souped up at the mission off Meyer Street
back in Tucson. When I told him I hadn't eaten since Dallas, he
made me drink some more water.

"I suspicioned that was it, Pancho," he mumbled. "When
you're on the scuffle long enough you can tell when a stiff hasn't
eaten." His heavy face seemed darker with some sort of worry,
and he kept glancing anxiously at me.

"Pancho, we'll quit this man the first time he holes up so
you can load up," he said. "But you got to drink plenty of water
—it ain't good for a stiff to postpone breakfast, dinner, and supper for so long." He pillowed my head on a croker sack bulging
with bedding and clothes. "I punished myself when I was young,
too," he recalled. "I was too bashful to panhandle then."

The redball hummed the high-speed track's heavy rails
without slowing. It stayed on the hot rail and never went into the
hole. The noise of rolling cars rumbled and the rails vibrated. The
water was gone before we got to Picacho and the skin under my
beard felt raw and hot. But the burly rover swabbed my temples
until I fell asleep. I dozed fitfully dreaming about devils standing
on hot coals and sizzling in their own thick fat.

When I woke up we were in Casa Grande and the train was
slowing for a red block. Its thunder diminished like the roll of
a muffled drum, and the burly rover stood up and waited for the

jangle that would mean the engineer was giving the air brakes all
the pressure they could stand. When the jangle came, he helped
me off the train.

"Pancho, now we'll get you something more than air to
chaw on," he promised. "It won't be hard to scuffle up something—this weather's good for bottle-hustling. It'll be good
hittin' here."

He led me to the railroad depot water fountain and told
me to drink all I could hold. Then he made me lie down under
the water tank next to the Southern Pacific tracks.

"Now I'll get the eggs before the rabbits eat them," he
said. "You stay in the shade 'cause it's hotter than Hell with
the door shut."

After that he went out to hustle soda bottles worth four
cents apiece at groceries. He walked away with stately caution.
I watched him cross the highway that split the desert city like a
bright ribbon. The paralleling street was like the hump of an ant
bed, and into it people were pouring. It looked like Saturday, but
in this Arizona town the cotton chopping season was on.

The burly rover was gone almost two hours. Engrossed in
square-meal daydreams, I waited. When he came back, the sun
was high and along the highway the heat glimmered up from the
paving. He held up a sack filled with bread, milk, and cheese
when he saw me. He said he'd found nineteen soda bottles, and
sold them all at a Mom and Pop grocery.

"I scored in the alleys and along the road shoulders," he
said. "Scoff it up, Pancho—it'll take the wrinkles out of your
belly."

Then he put his calloused hand under my chin, and tilted
the milk carton so I could drink. I drank the milk and wolfed
down the food. I don't remember tasting it. But after I had
eaten, I felt strength in the breadth of my chest and the slope of
my shoulders, in the steadiness of my legs, and the firmness of
my stomach. I thanked the burly rover and asked why he'd taken
on trouble that wasn't his.

He didn't reply right away. He studied me with a scholar's
slow scrutiny for a moment, and I remember the way his fierce

black moustaches stood straight out past his weathered cheeks. But the moustaches only were fierce about him, for his smile when he spoke to me was mild and wide and showed white teeth and his voice was soft and full.

"Pancho, a stiff ain't himself when he's hungry—he's liable to steal," was his answer. "And I wouldn't want to see a young field tramp do that when I could make a hustle to help him."

After that we looked for a good catchout place so we could nail another westbound drag.

HUNGRY MEN

In Gila Bend, I jungled up on the desert with a lanky, sway-backed rover whose clothes were so ragged he had them tied on with binder twine.

The grayness that comes at four-thirty found us half-frozen and we headed for the SP tracks with our train-riding cardboards under our arms.

We plodded ankle-deep through the soft earth of a pasty dust road toward the picket of telephone poles that marked the highway. The chill wind whipped up a smoke dust that made our lips leathery, and the lanky rover began breathing like he had been running.

He walked with an irregular, rocking gait, and swayed slightly on his heels. His gray eyes stared with little focus, and he had to stop and catch his breath. When his breathing became easier, he told me he'd souped up at the Bakersfield Rescue Mission three days before, and that was the last time he'd eaten.

"The Bible guys give you two bowls of soup there if you swallow the first one in a hurry, and then you can take your time with the second," he said. "I wish I'd loaded up with more bread though—on the rough a stoop labor stiff never knows when he'll eat again and you got to take advantage of every score."

Hunger put a wobble in his legs, and the skin about his mouth began twitching. His coat blew loosely in the wind, and he moved with the uncertain slowness of the sick.

"I got to rest, Buddy," he said.

We sprawled out in the horseweeds near the highway, and he told me he'd made it in Bakersfield until the handle broke off the pump.

"I was makin' it scrapin' ground cotton and sleepin' in the labor contractor's truck off Cottonwood Road," he said. "But his wife was a religious woman and she seen me drag a jug in once or twice to keep from freezing so she made him put me out—it's been hit, run, and miss for me ever since."

He said he'd panhandled in Yuma, but got more bawlings-out than scores.

"I scared one woman—I had a beard and she must have thought I was a grizzly bear," he said. "Then I tried to put the rings on one of them businessmen, who take down big scores every day, but he growled. I said: 'Mister, could you'—then he growled and told me he made his working and wouldn't piece off no tramp. That made me mad and I said: 'Mister, I've heard men with high-grade educations call other men tramps and winos, but if you talk to them stiffs and study their history, you're liable to think different about them.'"

Light filtered over the eastern horizon and, like thinning smoke paling, the night faded into faint shadows. Somewhere a car screeched at a turn, and then rumbled on to fade into a singing murmur. Then an engine motor exploded and a truck's gears shot the sound of steel into the air. A huge red truck, filling almost half the highway, approached from the west. When the truck passed, the canvas over its cargo flapped and we could see apples piled up.

The lanky rover's face was sunken and the bones seemed about to break through the taut skin. But when he saw the apples, his long, bony face brightened and he threw back his head and laughed. He chuckled until the truck became a comma in the distance—a red point with a tail of dust.

"One of them apples would rattle in my empty belly like shot in a dishpan," he said.

*   *   *

Another night I rode a Nickel Plate freight train into Cleveland when the temperature was twelve below.

When I quit the train near the Cuyahoga River, there was very little feeling in my feet, and my legs were so stiff I could take steps only a few inches long.

A sleeted wind was blowing up from the river, and I had to rub my chest to stop the shivers. After that I jumped up and down on the roadbed's gravel ballast until the blood hurt in my arms, face, and feet. But I wasn't cold long.

A one-armed hobo, bundled up in a horse-blanket overcoat and wearing a faded cap turned down in earmuffs, was boiling coffee in an open tin at the Kingsbury Run hobo jungle. When he saw me, he invited me to warm up.

"It's a great life if you don't get the measles," he observed pleasantly when I hurried up to the chunk fire.

The one-armed hobo's creased face was pinched small with the cold and his eyes were red veined and deep in their sockets as if they had been pushed in. He looked the way men come to look when they eat at missions and sleep out in the cold, and he studied me while I dry-washed my hands over the slow fire.

"Son, you'll never die of brain fever," he concluded after looking at me for some time. "A number-one tramp would have better sense than to deck a flying saucer boxcar when the snow's knee-high to a ten-foot dog."

He asked how long I'd held down the speedball. When I told him I'd beaten my way from Terre Haute, he allowed it was lucky I hadn't frozen.

"Be luckier still 'n drink some coffee with me," he invited.

We took turns sipping the scalding coffee, and the one-armed hobo told me how he lost his left arm.

"I was standing on a flatcar in the Chowchilla yards about two years ago when the train jerked and threw me between the cars," he said. "I just barely got my head out from under the wheels, but wasn't quick enough to get my arm out. I been gimpin' around on sore feet doing leaf work and living on the world's mercy ever since. Build a fire, make coffee, wait for a train—that's my life now. Before that I was a crop hand—a good one."

The wind blowing hard from the northwest made a high whining sound around the corners of the sided boxcars on the rusty spur track that branched out nearby. A drag highballed through with a screech of its whistle and a brief clatter of wheels across the switch locks. The ground vibrated strongly when it thunderclapped past.

The one-armed hobo hunched his shoulders a little, pulled his overcoat collar higher around his throat, and edged closer to the chunk fire. He moved his spindly shoulders back and forth to work up a little warmth, and breathed on his hand to warm it. Then he looked up at me with slow languor.

"You haven't sunk into bummery yet have you, son?" he asked. "I'm still in it and I'll never get out."

His brows contracted and he clenched his hand until it was white, like paper.

"When you're down on your luck you got to ask them for it—they can't read your mind," he said. "But it's hard for me to beg—awful hard. You give everything away when you beg on the street—you got to stand there and take whatever they say to you. It's like a' old-whiskers tramp told me—you come into the world crawlin' 'n you're gonna crawl some more before you leave it."

The fire had lowered and its glow filtered the darkness like a luminous screen. There was a drag on the right-of-way and the switch engine that had just cut out a few cars was chugging in a cloud of steam on a siding. The cut cars were still rolling down a blind track where the switch engine had butted them. The road engine, with blasts of the whistle, called in the flagmen and the switchmen, and then tested her air.

"I never culled my jobs—I'd chop cotton, cut grapes, or thin sugar beets," the one-armed hobo said. "I went all out on jobs I liked like picking apples—I never minded carrying ladders half as big as telephone poles. I used to like to cut broccoli because you can straighten and stand up ever' so often—it ain't so hard on your back. I was a good fruit picker, too—that's cause I was fast with my hands.

"I took the road fever early—I started freight trainin' back in the boomer days when tramping was in style, and I never let many jobs get by me. I was a coast-to-coaster—I never could sit still very long. Sometimes I'd get a hundred dollars and go off the rail for a while, but it was like a lion dreaming of being tame and I always went back. A stiff's got to keep moving—only the lizards stay in the same caves until they die."

A fast passenger train rattled over the yard's intersecting rails, and we heard the trailing whistle that always means a train is balling along. The broken lights of the coaches flickered past, and we had a brief glimpse of diners, sleepers, and men smoking in a club car. Then the night closed in again, and the one-armed hobo said he didn't have the heart to go downtown and try for what he needed.

"I been a good scuffler, but I ain't got the vinegar to work women's hearts on Euclid Avenue tonight," he said.

We huddled by the fire waiting for dawn. Winking signal lights made the mainline's steel cross-tracks shimmer. The drag was still on the line waiting to go out, and the yardmaster, or somebody else who wore a trench coat, was making a last-minute check of the little white slips of paper tacked on the sides of the cars.

"Ain't no use for me to get sobby—I just got to keep scufflin'n things is bound to get better," the one-armed hobo mumbled tonelessly. "God meant for me to lose my arm, and the railroads never did ask me to ride their freight trains. Besides that the railroad give me six hundred dollars when I got out of the hospital—I had money to put on the wood then."

He shivered and his face grew reminiscent.

"That was a lot of money wasn't it, son," he said. "I never had six hundred dollars before."

SOMETHING ABOUT FIELDHANDS

In Bakersfield, I lined up at Nineteenth and M with dozens of other fieldhands waiting for day hauler's buses to carry them out to the pea fields.

A full-bearded fieldhand, called Raggedy Man on account of his torn clothes, waited with me. When I told him I'd just come in from Stockton, he smiled and allowed I'd arrived just in time for the harvest. But when I asked how the peas were, he frowned.

"It's been too cold—peas need warm weather and they're not filling up like they should," he said. "They aren't going to be swollen like they were last year. Buddy, we made it good then. Stiffs were earning their six or seven dollars a day. You could see jungle fires all along that spur track behind the San Joaquin Cotton Oil Company at night. Field tramps were cooking up, and it was nice to see everyone getting enough to eat. But it's not like that this year on account of the rains. There's a lot of hungry blanket stiffs running up and down the railroad tracks, and if I'm lying my elbow's named Dennis."

It was cold and frosty, and the wind blew steadily from the north. We sat down on the curb near Uncle Dave's Pawnshop, and the Raggedy Man said there hadn't been much field work in Kern County since the carrots.

"I been sleeping in a condemned boxcar on a spur track just off the Edison Highway," he said. "And I been living mostly on potatoes that Pacific Fruit Express icemen sweep out of reefers when they clean them. That's pride-breaking eating, but a stiff's not himself when he's hungry."

Another fieldhand, small, pale, and nicknamed Shades because he wore pinch-nose glasses, sat down beside us on the curb. He had a pinched, bony face, and there were tired circles under his eyes. He drew his breath in convulsive jerks, making a sharp whistling sound against his teeth, and each exhalation was like the sudden deflation of a balloon. He said he'd hustled soda bottles all winter.

"Groceries pay four cents for every empty bottle," he said. "One day I walked clear to Greenfield looking for bottles on the road shoulders. I found eighteen and that meant 72 cents so I bought four pounds of pinto beans, and still had twelve cents left over for snuff. But it's hard to scuffle up something—the weather's cold for bottle-hauling."

The dim-lighted thoroughfare of small cafes, walkup hotels, and dingy scuffle joints, hummed like a running belt with the voices of many fieldhands. A cheery man, wearing a gray rope sweater, a faded brown derby and mud-caked gabardine trousers patched with Durham sacks, shook hands with the Raggedy Man. His good-natured face was fiery red from the wind, and he said he'd topped carrots and then sold whole blood and plasma on LA's Nickel Street skid row after Kern County's field work gave out.

"Field tramping hasn't hurt me any—I don't look a day over 200," he said.

A day hauler's bus with WILLIAM BLEVINS stenciled on its blue sides nosed into the curb, and a lanky, red-haired bull-horn bawled: "Let's get those peas, men—let's make that farmer go to the bank at ten o'clock in the morning."

The street livened up. Fieldhands milled around the parked bus with heads lowered to keep the whistling wind from cutting their faces.

"I'll be glad when winter's over," the Raggedy Man mumbled. "I'd rather hunt a shade than a stove."

It was growing lighter. The sky was gray in the east and the moon had set, but the half-dark city was still only faintly streaked with daylight. The farm bus began to fill up.

Shades blinked sleepily when he got on the bus, and his breathing was like a sigh.

"I'm sleepier than Rip Van Winkle, and I wouldn't get on this bus at all if it wasn't for Mr. Need More," he averred. "You know him don't you, buddy? He's the guy that loads these farm buses. It don't matter though. This'll be country gravy compared to what I've went through this winter."

* * * *

The stocky, barrel-chested fieldhand picking peas in the next row filled his hamper about the same time I did. He straightened up, grimacing from the strain on his back, calves, and thighs.

"Easy money ain't it, Pancho? he remarked pleasantly.

Away ahead, in the distance, a long range of sharp hills embroidered the horizon. Wind-driven clouds raced before a smoky blob that seemed to pursue them. The wind's chill crawled under my trouser cuffs and down the neck of my collar and I turned up my lapels.

"Wind's about to blow away the mortgage on the widow's old cow," the stocky man said.

He had a handkerchief tied like a mask over his nose and mouth to keep out the dust. He closed his teeth down over his lower lip, and kept his head bent while he untied it. After that we hefted the hampers to our shoulders, and plodded toward the grading bins. There was a long line ahead of us, and we waited our turn while graders culled out short, flat, and spotted pea pods.

The stocky man rolled a cigarette down between his knees, where the wind couldn't get at it, and then passed the makings to me. After that, with his mouth and nostrils dense with smoke, he rewrapped his sack of tobacco and matches in waxed bread paper and put it back in his shirt pocket. He had a strong candid face with mild eyes, and his hair was like pulled taffy in streaks and gray for the rest of it. He wore a peanut straw haying hat, and it was pushed back on his brows. Occasionally he would show his teeth in a slow smile. After a while he told me he'd been a coal miner in Hazard, Kentucky, before his wife died. He talked without gestures, and without opening his lips very far.

"After she died I went to field tramping," he said. "That was two years ago, and I been on a ramble ever since."

The long line thinned out. We moved on to the grading bins, and the stocky man said he'd stayed with his married son in Houston part of the winter.

"My son's a longshoreman, and a fine boy," he said. "He works mostly trimming grain and sulphur, some cotton and washdown jobs too. He treated me about as nice as a father could ask. He threw up his hand and said goodbye to me when he went to work every morning, and he bought me instant coffee and Prince Albert. Beside that I had two changeovers of clothes. That boy didn't want to see me leave. He said: 'Don't go, Dad—stay here with me and Constance.' I'd have liked to have stayed, but I knew it wouldn't be right. So I said to him: 'Son, if I was disabled I'd stay but I'm able to make it. I got to go—I can't set down on you no longer.'"

The graders culled out our bad peas, and we moved on to the scales and waited in line for a weigh-up. The sky had begun to spot with rain, and the wind had come up stronger. We could hear far off in the distance the occasional whistle of a freight train which, dying down, left the field quiet again.

"After I left my boy's house I went out to the SP yards and got on a through Man, and hung it to Yuma," the stocky man said. "Then I got on another fast fellow, and I doubled back to Phoenix, I made the day hauls in the carrots and stayed in a double-decker flophouse on Jefferson Street. But the Sweet Lucy's went to juggin' and fussin' all night so I moved out and slept in that jungle stiffs call the Icehouse. Before long farm work slacked up though, and I couldn't catch a day haul. They was tying onions by then, and the day haulers left a whole lot of hands behind. So I went to the soupline at St. Vincent de Paul's on Ninth Avenue. I counted 356 in the soupline that day, not including women and children. So many lined up the meat was out of the stew when my turn come. After that I heard the peas was about ready so I come here. That was a beautiful ride from LA. That empty boxcar didn't bounce—just waved a little —it was a hydra-cushion car. Going over the hump it got cold though. I had three quilts and my overcoat, and when I woke up there was snow on me. But I snuggled down deeper, and kept warm."

The line thinned out again, and we carried our hampers to the scales. The weigh-hand was middle-aged with chapped, scaling lips, and a body that bulged in the middle like a top. He said we each had 25 pounds of peas, and we showed the paymaster our work cards. The paymaster had on clean khaki work clothing, and his clean-shaven face had a rich, healthy coloring. He wore a black Sam Browne belt, and his pistol was pearl-handled. He marked our work cards, and paid us. After that we went back to our rows.

Rain was falling lightly now, like mist. The stocky man set down his hamper and then pulled up his foot, and examined the loosened sole of his field shoe.

"Ain't so bad as the short-handled hoe is it, Pancho," he said.

He smiled and fixed his eyes on me.

"I'd rather tough it out in this pea patch than live off my son, and just rock on his front porch," he said.

After that he bent almost double over the peavines again.

HOMELESS MAN

Boarding the Texas and Pacific freight train at Sweetwater I found an empty boxcar and swung from the car top through the open door. No one else was in the car and in the flare of a match I found a heavy woolen blanket in a corner. It was cold that night and dark clouds drifted low, whipped along by a slashing west wind that sent sand fogging into the air. When the cold penetrated my clothes I wrapped the blanket around me and I lay in a corner listening to the heavy exhaust of the three engines and the clacking of the wheels over rail joints. As the night got colder, I was glad the blanket had been there. I slept.

At Odessa the brakemen looked into the boxcar and found me. The flash of their lanterns woke me and I blinked when I opened my eyes. There were two of them and they smiled and asked if I'd had a rough ride. The TP was an easy road to beat then and a hobo could easily make the three divisions between Fort Worth and El Paso in one jump. On the TP no rail bulls would make me get off and wait for the next train. All I had to look out for was policemen.

The brakemen told me the train would stop at Odessa for about an hour. The prairie wind, fuller now, was still keening from the west and the moon was getting low. It must have been between two and three o'clock then.

I did not want to get up, but the brakemen said they were going to set off all the empties. It was a work train and more cars would be cut at Toyah, and Sierra Blanca. Only sealed cars and tri-levels were going on through to El Paso.

I thanked the brakemen for letting me know about that and then jumped out of the boxcar. I walked fast down the tracks toward the head-end of the train, and I heard footsteps following me. I looked back and one of the brakemen was looking into the rest of the cars, and a tall, swaybacked man was following me. He was wearing a slicker, and I heard it rustling with each step. He had a bandana tied around his forehead and he moved in uncertain, jerky steps like an infant traversing a wavering course from chair to chair. He kept his eyes on his feet and the chalky rock of the roadbed. I waited for him to catch up. His eyes were watering, and he looked pale and shaky. He spoke in Spanish, a greeting.

I said, *"Muy buenas noches, señor"* and smiled at him. Then I said something more in Spanish, a question, but this time he shrugged and spread his hands. For a long time he stood very still looking at me, and I could see he did not understand. Then he spoke slowly in English, trying to find small words I would understand.

"You go?" he asked, and pointed down the track toward the west.

"Si señor," I said. "El Paso."

He took his ragged hat off and dusted it across his legs, and then put it back on his head.

"You want coffee?" he asked, making a motion at his stomach to be sure I would understand what he meant.

I realized he thought I was a wetback. So, in accented English, I told him I would like coffee. He seemed pleased because I spoke some English. He smiled without parting his lips and then said he knew other Spanish words beside *"como sigue."* but they were mostly swear words.

"I learned some Spanish from hearing Mexicans talk in the farm labor camps," he explained.

To repay him for inviting me to have coffee, I offered him the blanket I had found. When he realized I was giving him the blanket, he turned his pockets out for me, offering me what he had. He talked brokenly in English himself and kept offering me tobacco, a carpenter's trimming knife with a broken blade and two pennies.

Then he smiled and said *"gracias cuate"* again and again and he took the blanket and led me to a wood fire burning between two piles of bricks on the prairie near a rusty spur track overgrown with weedstalks.

There was a bed of red coals in the fire with ashes banked up around them to keep them from rolling out. Nearby was an old cottonwood with storm-broken boughs and strewn around it were a few cracked and broken vegetable crates. The tall man went after a crate. He came back and scraped the embers together and placed the crate carefully on the fire. The fire crackled. It turned yellow and light filled the jungle.

By then the wind had sloped to the northwest and had flattened to an even blowing. Mesquite trees and bear grass clumps that had bent over and sprung up now leaned one way under a steady pressure. The wind's chill crawled under my trouser cuffs and down the neck of my collar and I turned up the lapels. I hovered over the burning vegetable crate trying to get warm while the tall man boiled coffee in a tincan. He had made a holder from some rusty wire, and he held the tincan over the fire with it. When the coffee was boiling, he looked at me. His eyes were red-veined from the wind.

"Pancho, it's cold and this coffee will grab hold of you," he said. "You'll be ready to cross the desert on your burro."

The coffee was bitter but hot, driving out the morning chill. We took turns sipping it, and the tall man said he couldn't do row-crop work any more.

"I got arthritis in both knees," he said. "I can't get down and draw my feet up under me like I used to. My legs give way on me. They don't go where I want them."

He picked up a small, dry stick and began to tap it on his leg.

"I don't have no choice, but to stay at missions now," he said. "I got to stay close to the souplines. I'm just trying to stay alive until I get my old-age pension. It's a hard way to live, lots of roughage. I don't get homesick for field work though."

He hunched his shoulders as if he were chilled and hugged his slicker closer about him. Then he reached into both pockets of the slicker. From one pocket he drew out several partially-smoked cigarettes, from the other a match. He tried to light one of the cigarettes, but it was too short and he threw it away.

"I was riding a east guy when I got set off here along about midnight," he said. "The train stopped and they cut off a few empties. I was asleep in one of those empties all newspapered up and I had my shoes off. By the time I got them on the engines had coupled up and that east guy had gone out without me. There's good hanging-out places around these yards though so I built this fire and piled up some tumbleweeds to keep the wind off me. There won't be another hotshot until tonight. There's a load goes right on through to Fort Worth then."

A road engine purred beyond the toolhouse waiting to hook onto the drag. I went after another vegetable crate and put it on the fire. The fire was burning well and one crate did not last very long.

"This is hard-up country, but Odessa's a good stop," the tall man said. "They got a good feeding mission here. They serve family-style, and you can pitch until you win. That preacher and his wife set right down and eat with the stiffs. It's three miles from these east yards, but they feed you like mother did. They really put it on the table. I'll eat there tonight and then come back here and hang that east guy if I don't get lawed for loitering first."

He held his eyes down, watching the toes of his scarred shoes. His shoes were big and black, with flat heels and round toes, the high, old-fashioned type lacing all the way up to the instep. Looking down at them his face changed, not the movement of muscles, but a withdrawing of a human, warm quality.

"I've been in and out of so many jails I can't recall their names," he said. "It don't look like I can stay out, but I don't do nothing to get in there. I got lawed in El Paso—that's a tough stop. I was going to the Rescue Mission on San Francisco Street, and I was carrying a moving van pad tied with haywire. Those moving van pads are good to ride trains on. They're so big you can lay down on one side of them and cover yourself with the other. Rolled up they're bundlesome though and they'll attract a Town Clown's attention. So this crime combat car with two Mexican laws in it pulled up alongside me and one of them gave me a growl. 'Hey you, where you going?' he asked me. 'I'm looking for a place to stay,' I said. 'Come on, we'll give you one,' he said. Then he kicked me and why I don't know. I never said nothing to him. I oughtn't to have carried that moving van pad along North Oregon Street though. You got to be all jellied up and have a good address to stay out of trouble in these cities. Anybody who's been off the farm for a week knows that."

The words had been pouring from him like a relieving flood of tears, but now, with disconcerting abruptness, he stopped. He stirred the fire with a stick, sending sparks swirling up with the smoke. Then he looked at me and smiled apologetically.

"Except for those two laws, Mexicans have always helped me," he said. "In Tucson I was so sick I could hardly walk from the SP yards to the mission at Twenty-Eighth Street and Ninth Avenue. I went into this Mexican cafe and said to the waitress, 'Lady, I'm running a fever and I got chills. Could I set down for awhile?' She said, 'Mister you just set down as long as you want,' and she brought me caldo and coffee. Then last year in San Antonio I went into this Mexican bakery near the Katy yards on South Flores Street and I told the woman, 'Lady, just give me a dime's worth of those cupcakes and pastries.' She filled up a sack and started filling up another and I said, 'Lady, I just wanted a dime's worth.' She laughed and said, 'Mister, you don't have it yet.'"

He looked down the tracks, as if fleetingly suspicious of an unseen hazard. Dark patches of color under his eyes gave him a cavernous appearance. He slipped his hands inside the waistband of his trousers, palms inward, and stood with elbows jutting sharply outward.

"I'll be glad when winter's over," he said. "I'd rather hunt a shade than a stove. I been living like a poor old outcast dog, but I'll make it better when summer comes. I'll be 65 then and I'll go back home to Missouri and try for a state 'old' check there. Some oldtimers get more than seventy dollars a month."

The wind was blowing and rattling the brush and the fire was flickering and making shadows. He turned up the collar of his slicker and watched the sparks fly up and go out.

"When my 'old' check comes in I'll get straight," he said. "I'll build me a 12x12 shack on a quarter section of family farm land near Crowderville. I'll get me a lantern and shoot a squirrel of a morning and fish for clawhead catfish. I'll sell them for twenty-five cents apiece when I get the money for trot lines. You meal them and salt them good and ain't nothing like them. I'm going back among friends where I can say, 'John, how's the family?' "

He took a deep breath, relaxed, and then straightened his thin shoulders. He smiled, his head slightly thrust forward, revealing the face of a tired pilgrim, ill and worn, who has come within sight of his goal. He spoke in a voice scarcely above a whisper, as a man talks to himself.

"I'll live so I don't have to jump from my own shadow," he said.

THE GRAY-HAIRED MAN

The gray-haired man with the rubber-tipped cane and slow, painful gait said he was walking in the direction of the railroad yards himself and would show me the way. I did not mind his slow gait. It was Sunday morning and Fort Worth's quiet streets were only streakily illuminated by daylight. The morning sun was so faint behind the clouds that the wintry day seemed like gray twilight.

We walked along West Vickery Street, and the gray-haired man said he'd left Brother Bill's Mission without eating the night before. He explained why.

"Brother Bill may be holy, but he damned sure ain't friendly," he said. "He preached that same old long sermon about how God told him to spit out his cigarette, put away his jug, and walk down the King's Highway. 'I'm a sinner saved by grace,' he said. 'Will you say Amen to that all you evil Adamites that go to churches that compromise?' Then when he got through preaching, he said, 'Now how many men want to be saved? All who haven't been saved raise their hands. Come to God—you've got nothing to lose. You're sinning out on the road.' Didn't nobody but a couple of old mission stiffs raise their hands though, and that made him mad. 'You bums have it good here,' he said. 'Where would you be tonight if we didn't let you stay here? You'd be out begging in the streets. How many homes would be opened to you tonight? Most would cast you out. You should thank God there are good Christians who take you into this mission. When three more come to God you can eat.'"

He shivered; to control his shivering he moved his shoulders and beat his right hand up against his chest. For a while it helped, but he could not beat fast enough, and long shivers began to run down his body where the raw wind hit him.

"I'd rather beg in the streets than listen to that kind of talk just for a bowl of soup with maybe seven beans in it," he said. "So I just up and walked to the door. When I walked away, I heard Brother Bill shout, 'It got too hot for that man. He was afraid he might be saved.' But I went out the door anyway."

We passed plain frame houses with cold, clipped lawns and beds of stiff flower stalks, and the gray-haired man said he'd slept in a doorknocker's junk truck.

"After I walked out of Brother Bill's Mission, I saw these two junk trucks parked right next to each other, and one of them had a blanket in it," he said. "So I got into it quiet and nested down and didn't smoke. After a while I heard another stiff get into the junk truck next to mine and he started smoking and coughing. Pretty soon I heard a man holler, 'Hey you, get the hell out of there.' So the stiff had to get up and go. But I wasn't coughing so nobody noticed me. That's why I don't smoke in trucks. It makes you cough and you got to be quiet."

He spoke in a tired voice without even raising his eyes. He was small and very thin. His bones showed everywhere and his face looked worn and gaunt. The heightening wind, strong as a squall, flattened his gray hair against his head, and his shirt collar billowed out from his stringy neck. His clothes were shapeless from being slept in and the left sleeve of his coat was empty, pinned against the coat and tucked into the side pocket. He smiled when I looked at it.

"I'm not so bad off, Pancho," he said. "I can shave myself and roll a cigarette good as the next boabout. But if I buy tailor mades I have a hard time breaking the cellophane open."

We crossed the empty street, and the gray-haired man said he'd been a boomer cook in skid row cafes before he lost his left arm. Since then he'd picked pole beans, scrapped ground cotton and sold blood. What hurt him most he said, was losing the arm he cooked with.

"That hurt me, Pancho, because I'm left-handed," he said. "I just used my right hand to pick up pots and pans with. It's a hard get-by now. I'm like a dog keeping house in an alley. I miss cooking, Pancho. I'd rather be over a stove with a spatula than any place else I know. I worked in cafes where they served 1500 meals a day and didn't nobody ever say I was too slow. People said all kinds of nice things about my cooking. When I worked at Big Mama's Cafe on Two Street in Sacramento she told everyone I was the best butter bean cook she ever seen and bragged about how fast I chopped vegetables with the French knife and how well I mashed potatoes."

He smiled, his gaunt face creasing at the sides of his mouth, and his pale eyes grew reminiscent.

"I never cooked in a place off the skid row, but once I washed dishes at a big hotel in Miami Beach," he said. "The dishwashing machine made it easy. I made seven dollars a day and ate everything on the order, even steaks. But I got restless and quit. A red-headed hostess asked me to stay. She was a nice lady. She said, 'You got it good here. You can eat all you want, and you got a six dollar-a-day room.' The waitresses were nice to me, too."

The Mexican boy pulling the cart with a big black cazuela of menudo looked at us, but did not pause. The dog beside him was so old he didn't trot. He just walked step by step like an old man. We walked west slowly. The street was beginning to look shabbier. Most of the houses needed painting; the shingled roofs had a dingy, weather-beaten look. "I've sold a lot of blood since I lost my left arm," the gray-haired man said. "I carry my blood type in my pocket—it's A-Positive. By rights a rough-work stiff shouldn't have to sell blood to get something to eat though. If you were giving blood to another stiff that was dying it would be different, but selling it just don't seem right. I keep putting down though because I'm hungry most of the time."

The chilly wind swept across the tops of the cottonwoods, shaking the massed branches. The wind stiffened the beard stubble on my cheeks, and I worked my mouth so it wouldn't feel so rigid. The gray-haired man hummed gently through his teeth and watched leaves, which had lost their green, whirl down to the ground.

"I sell blood because I can't panhandle," he said. "As long as I've been on the blink I've never been able to panhandle. A stiff's not normal or average when he's hard-pressed, but I hit it the rough way. I never learned how to ask, and I can't hardly walk up to a man and ding-dong him. When you're hungry you got to go out and greet them. They won't bring it to you. But I couldn't bum salt. If I tried to panhandle, the second guy I'd brace would be a law. I've been so hungry I couldn't hardly talk and I've thought maybe some man might help me get a sandwich, but when I walk up to them I fade away and my courage fails me. I'll go hungry until we get to Big Spring, and then I'll get something to eat at the Sally. You can double up on that stew there after the ear-binging's over."

It was getting colder. The wind blew through my windbreaker and flannel shirt and I seemed to feel it pressing on my ribs. The gray-haired man raised his hand stiffly and pulled his coat collar up around his neck. But he was chilled through, and he could not stop shivering. His teeth kept chattering together and the cold seemed to run up through his body, making his arm shake. He went on doggedly putting one foot carefully in one square of the sidewalk, then lifting the other foot and putting it carefully in one square ahead.

We neared the Round House Cafe, just north of the Texas and Pacific yards. There was a flat, broken stretch of dumping ground studded with signboards and clumps of dead weeds alongside the washboard road that led to the yards, and off beyond the broken ground the smoke of the roundhouse streaked low in the sky.

"I hope we can find a open," the gray-haired man said. "I hope everything rolling ain't sealed. There's a hotshot comes in from St. Louis at eleven o'clock and this is the only place they switch him. That hotshot don't usually carry any empties though. He's usually got a load, all sealed cars and car haulers. So we'll have to hang that Man they make up in the yards. He goes out on Rail Number One, that track they call the West Bowl, and I hope it's a long train. When he pulls a long train there's lots of good places to ride."

There were no bull cars on the washboard road. We turned down it, and the gray-haired man told me how he lost his left arm.

"I was standing on a flatcar in the Great Northern hump yards at Seattle about five years ago when the train jerked and threw me between the cars," he said. "I just barely got my head out from under the wheels, but I wasn't quick enough to get my arm out. I saw a car knocker and a brakeman turn their faces away when the wheels went over it, but I didn't moan or cry out. It didn't hurt any—it was just a dead feeling. When the trainmen got me to the hospital my arm was just hanging by a shred, but it still didn't hurt any until a doctor took it off. Then the nerve hit me, I guess, and it was like a electric shock in my back and all over my body. But I still didn't moan any. The doctor put his hand on my shoulder and said, 'Buddy, you got more guts than any man I ever seen.' Yeah, that's what he told me, Pancho."

The memory must have meant a great deal to him—just a moment ago he had been trembling with hunger and cold, now his voice was even and calm. His thoughts seemed to have left no room for the cold and hungry day's troubles, and when he spoke it was from a great distance with his pale eyes turned inward. "After the doctor left I began bawling though, Pancho," he said. "I could have stood the pain in silence, but I just kept crying and moaning."

He looked at me and smiled wanly. "I guess even a ferocious beast will break down and bawl sometimes," he said.

NIGHT TRAIN TO FORT WORTH

One night I got on a Texas and Pacific mainline run at Toyah with a one-legged rover nicknamed Sticks because of his crutches. When the engineer eased the train out, picking up the slack without a bump, we were in an empty with open laths about six cars behind the Big Jack engine.

A damp soft snow was falling, and we bundled up with carlining. But the wind blowing straight and steady from the northwest made us feel the snow's wetness on our foreheads. Sticks, small and spindly with a gray-streaked beard that didn't hide his sickly complexion, shivered.

"You feel the cold more when you're hungry, buddy," he mumbled apologetically.

Near Pecos the freight train thundered over a highball stretch so fast it skipped on rail joints, and the rocking boxcars hit back on their coupling pins with a wrenching jerk. We sat with our legs apart and our heads down, bracing for sudden jolts of slack, with our hips numb from the pounding. Then the train began to bounce with a staccato roll, and we stood up to ease the punishment. The double-track roadbed was speeding away beneath us, and the barren alkali land swung in a semicircle around the boxcar's metal door. Sticks lurched forward, but the train jarred him straight. He blinked owlishly, and showed his worn-down teeth in a grin.

"This boxcar's like a leaping tuna—it's got eight flat wheels and should have gone to the shops a hundred years ago," he said.

When the boxcar's jarring rattle lessened, we bundled up with carlining again and Sticks, shivering in a raveled rope sweater with the collar turned up around his face, told me he'd sold blood plasma in Los Angeles.

"My arm's like a dopehead's with needle marks—I was puttin' down twice a week there," he said. "I was blowin'n goin' though—I eat one of those 51-cent meals at Jake's on the Nickel Street skid row every day and I slept warm in that tramp dormitory above the Hard Rock Bar at Fifth and Wall every night. That plasma's a good deal—it ain't like the four-dollar blood banks. You can give it twice a week, and they never take the needle out of your arm. They get the plasma and then put your blood back in and give you dextrose besides. It takes about a hour—like a operation. But the last time I went to the Plasma Center they turned me down—not enough iron. It don't matter though—I'll make it better in Texas. Where there's hundreds of stiffs waiting in L.A. souplines there's only dozens in Fort Worth."

Out in the open the wind was blowing harder and the snow was getting heavier. The train was running faster, and the suction scooped up cinders from the roadbed and pelted them against the steel cars. Sticks rolled up his sleeve and showed his biceps. His arm at the elbow was pockmarked with little white dots.

"A nurse give me a bottle of iron tablets," he said. "I taken all those tablets so I'll be ready to sell blood again in Fort Worth. I'll bleach the four-dollar blood bank's finger marks off with Clorox so I won't have to wait six weeks to put down again and then make the Plasma Center too. If I'm still low on iron I'll go to Scotty's Blood Bank—they just take your temperature and a sample and don't ask no questions there. Me'n you'll fill up with Oklahoma-style black eyes when I get my passover money. You can make it in Fort Worth, buddy—you're on both feet."

He passed me a tobacco sack and one of the brown paper bags that hoboes roll cigarettes with when they run out of the regular book tissues. After that he rolled a cigarette himself, packing the tobacco carefully so no grain would fall and then guiding his lips along the edge of the bag of paper with his forefinger.

"I been on the rail all my life—I got to hear that train

rolling and the wheels clicking," he said. "Hardships ain't broke me of the habit—I was born with a goin' spell and I got rambling in my blood. When I make up my mind to go with my back roll and skillet I'll ride any kind of a load. I got it from my daddy—he was a horse trader in Antlers, Oklahoma, and went around from place to place. Once I tried to get off the tracks and I worked at the pay desk in a big walk-up flophouse that had 300 wire cages. But I quit because I had to climb a section ladder and pick fruit so I could eat and sleep good—just settin' was killing me. I've gandied and sawmilled and worked on ranches too—that's how I lost my leg last year. A steer kicked me and broke it in two places."

The train's thunder rolled, and a wire fence beside the tracks took up the vibration and hummed with it. A truck passed on the narrow, high-centered highway paralleling the railroad's high embankment and there was the sound of milk bottles clattering in a tin rack. Then the roadbed turned on a banking curve and down the tracks we could see a highway town's hazy lights, clean and beautiful in the snow. The strung colored lights of this town's main street illuminated an empty, quiet thoroughfare. The stores were closed; the depot dark. On the courthouse lawn a big lighted Christmas tree glowed greens and reds and yellows. The sign at the edge of the sleeping town read: *Fort Worth. . . 310 miles*. Sticks compressed his lips and closed his eyes.

"After I lost my leg I tried peddling needles I bought for seven cents a box from wholesalers in San Francisco," he said. "But the Bay Area's hilly and you got to walk up eight or ten steps to a house. I got used to dogs barking and grabbing me by the britches-leg. But all that climbing with the sticks made my thigh gall me so, and my shoulders, knee, and ankle ache and hurt so much I had to give it up. After that I was hittin' it pretty rough. I was hungry and couldn't find a sleeping place so I had to carry the stick. One night I stopped to get warm in a bowling alley near Sacramento's two street skid row. But they could tell I was on the dog because I was raggedy and smelled of smoke so they run me out. After that I taken to selling my blood."

Monahans was a snow-blurred sprinkle of lights pushing toward us like a mammoth postcard. Just west of the town near an old, abandoned wildcat well, the freight train took the siding to let a westbound manifest pass and we stood in the boxcar's wide doorway looking out at the mesquite-clumped prairie. The mesquite trees were thick and made a fence for a clearing on which an old derrick rose. Its timbers were gray as an old mop; away from it a little piece lay a huge wooden bullwheel with rusty bolts.

Somewhere dogs were baying. It was a vibrant, sonorous sound like the musical notes of a deep reed instrument. Wind gushed in the trees with the sound of a distant river and the tops of the cottonwoods, silhouetted against the sky, whipped and threshed like tiny Christmas trees in a storm. The rails began to murmur and after a while a locomotive's light showed, tiny as a lightning bug. It began to swell and the earth trembled as if the railroad cut's sides were going to cave in and carry us under the train. Then the manifest's pounding wheels thundered and crashed and, after a long time, the red marker lights of the caboose passed. Sticks pinched off the burning end of his cigarette and, breaking the paper, poured the tobacco into a sack.

"I'm pretty well beat down, buddy, and I ought to get down on my knees for some help," he said. "But I'd rather be on my own and not on the mercy of missions. A stiff finds a little companionship running up and down the railroad tracks. On every train there's a new buddy to pal up with, and in every jungle there's a boabout going your way. I made it better during the depression though. The older you get the tougher it gets—people start calling you Pop."

The locomotive wheels spun slowly, pulling hard, and we could hear the coupling pins knocking against each other and connecting. Then the boxcars moved and the slack ran out of the drawheads. The freight train was going east again. The brown grass along the fence lines bent flat in the wind, and snow sprayed through the boxcar's latticed sides. Sticks shuddered and clenched his teeth. Beneath the white skin of his neck, the muscles were limp and trembling.

"The road gets in a man's blood, but there are times when he wants shelter and a roof over his head," he said. "I'd like to get me a little old tin and tarpaper shack near the railroad yards and just squat for a while. A hobo, when he ain't traveling, just likes to sit and watch yard engines work boxcars around."

He dropped his head to his chest and then came up straight with a shudder, jerking his closed eyes open.

"Soon's it gets warm I'll freight up to Sioux City. They pay twenty dollars a pint for O-Positive blood there," he said.

The locomotive whistle whined back through the snow.